CHARLIE'S TRIPS

Jack Felson is a French bilingual writer and filmmaker, born in 1970. He started writing in 1995 and could publish two collections of short stories, *After AIDS* (2002) in France, and *Four* (2006) in the United States.

Charlie's Trips is his first published novel.

CHARLIE'S TRIPS

by
Jack Felson

Two Colors

Published in 2011 by Two Colors Ventures, Ltd., London, United Kingdom

ISBN: 978-0-9565580-0-8

Printed and bound in the United States of America

Part

ONE

Somewhere in the city of Hot Springs, Arkansas, not far from the Oklahoma and Texas borders.

Tim Bradshaw, a 40-year-old muscular family man, climbed the stairs to the upper floor of his house and knocked on a closed door.

"Charlie, dinner time!" he said.

Inside the bedroom his eldest son, Charlie, 16, with short brown hair, was playing a video game, one of those taking the point of view of the hero and the heavy weapon he uses to shoot as many bad guys as possible. Charlie had the look of the typical schoolboy, and at this moment he was behaving exactly like the typical schoolboy. But he was not a schoolboy.

"Charlie, come down! I mean now!" Tim turned the handle. The door was locked. So he knocked again, harder. "Charlie! Open it or I break it open!"

"Oh please Dad! Two more minutes!" Charlie's voice sounded.

"Last call! You come down now or you spend the night starving!"

There was no other response, so Tim gave up; he turned and walked back downstairs.

The kid kept playing like nothing happened. Soon his dad came back.

"Hey kid, there's a war movie on TV!" he yelled.

Charlie heard it, he turned off his game at once, stood up, went to the door and opened it.

He found his father standing just in front of him, like some evil shape about to take him to some hell place.

"I was kidding," Tim said. He grabbed his son. "Now get your teen ass downstairs!" He dragged him downstairs, giving him no chance to turn loose and get back to his bedroom and video game.

Tim was far from doing this for the first time. He was the father of three; Charlie was his eldest child, and he was addicted to video games when the two others were not. This had made him the only one who needed to be regularly called more than once, and, if necessary, to be dragged by force to family meals and duties.

Since he'd left school he was always forgiven.

The rest of the Bradshaw family was waiting around the table as Tim finally appeared with Charlie, releasing him. Charlie put his collar back in place as he went to take his seat, facing his brother Kyle, 15, and sister Kathy, 13. Tim took his at one end of the table, facing his blonde, voluptuous wife Lorna, 38.

They started praying silently, saying nothing at

all. It was Lorna who moved her head up, finishing the praying show. "God Bless America," she said, crossing herself.

"God Bless America," Tim said in his turn. The three kids imitated them simultaneously.

Then they began eating. There were a couple of whisky bottles on the table. Only Tim, Lorna… and Charlie could touch them.

"How is it over there, Charlie?" Lorna asked.

"I told you, Mom, it's good. We have drills once a week, sometimes twice."

"What's a drill?" Kathy asked him.

"Well…"

His father gestured to him, making him silent.

"Oh come on, Daddy…" Kathy said.

"D'you wanna join the army or what?" Charlie said to her.

"Sure I do! I'll be a better soldier than you are!"

"Is she kidding?" Charlie said to his mother.

"Are you kidding?" she said to Kathy.

"Am I kidding?" Kathy asked Kyle.

"I guess not," Kyle said to Charlie.

"Sure you are," Charlie told Kathy.

"What's a drill?" Kathy asked him again.

"I'll tell you when you're bigger."

"I wanna know now!"

"You wanna eat." He gave her a plate of spaghetti, then a plate with the sauce, vegetables and meat in it, in order to keep her silent. "I still can tell you this," he said, "when you're a soldier you don't usually eat this well."

They all laughed, Kyle excepted, even if he kind

of agreed with what his brother had just said. The problem was he was on cold terms with Charlie since he had joined the army, when he was still at high school and was an example as a student. His almost perfect results at school weren't enough any more to attract the attention of his parents, who were feeling much prouder of Charlie than of him.

"Charlie, you're so cute," Lorna said.

"If you don't like the way they feed you," Kathy said, "why did you join them?"

"I didn't join them for the food. And you know what? I didn't join them for the drink, either!"

He laughed, picked up one of the whisky bottles and was about to drink from it when he stopped himself on time, poured the whisky in his glass and drank from it.

They looked at him with sorry eyes.

"I already knew you were a bloody pain in the neck," Kyle said, taking the opportunity, "now we all just found out you are a drunk one too."

"Let me tell you one thing, little brother," Charlie said. "At school, they teach you how to smoke. In the army, they all smoke already, so they teach you how to do other things. Like drink or do drugs. That's the way it is. You're a smoker, I can drink. Everyone has one vice and addiction. I don't call you some junkie, don't call me no drunk. Right? Thanks." He started eating again.

"Great speech," Kyle said ironically. "Who taught you that?"

"Nobody. I'm no school jerk any more."

"Easy boys, don't start again. Not here and

now," their dad said. "And Kyle, stop teasing your elder brother."

"I'm not," Kyle said. "He's teasing himself. Doesn't wanna be called a drunk when he drinks like a hole." Then, to Charlie: "And who told you I was smoking or drinking or doing drugs, smartass?"

"Kyle, what did I just say?"

"Sure you don't call me a junkie," Kyle continued, "I don't smoke or sniff anything."

"You're a liar," Charlie said.

"Grow up, big brother."

*

Two hours later, Tim, Lorna and Charlie were sitting on a couch in front of the television set, watching the news. There was something about attacks, bombings, robberies and some other general bad stuff. They watched this silently, more or less dismayed.

"When I see this it makes me proud of being a soldier and serving my country," Charlie said. "I mean, all this shit could happen in our city, close to our house!"

"You bet, son," Tim approved.

"Who does all this, in your opinion?" Lorna asked Charlie.

"One thing is sure," Charlie replied, "they're not American."

"You bet they ain't, son," Tim approved.

"They're everything but American, I mean, why

9

would fellow Americans bomb and rob their own country?"

His parents just looked at him, shrugging, then Tim said:

"There are many poor people in America, you know, son."

"That's not true. We never see any such people on TV."

"That's because they don't show them to us, Charlie. But they do exist," Lorna said. "Poor people, or addicted to some bad substances, who don't know what to do with their own lives. Most of them live out there on the streets. So lost that you can't imagine."

They kept watching the news, until a commercial break came up.

"Tell me son, how does it feel to be the youngest of all soldiers?" Tim asked.

"Well, it means something."

"What do your fellows over there think about that?" Lorna asked.

"Oh please, Mom."

"Tell your mom, son," Tim said.

"How can I know? There are so many of them. Some of them are friends of mine, some others are not, and I don't talk to the rest."

"Those who're not your friends, how tough are they on you?"

Without giving an answer, Charlie picked up the TV remote control. "God I hate those stupid comercials," he said. He started changing channels. "They're not my friends, Dad, that's all," he answered, while keeping working on the remote control. "It doesn't mean they're playing tough on me."

"Yeah but don't tell me there's nobody on you. I was in the army too, I know the rules out there."

Charlie ended up finding the movie *We Were Soldiers,* starring Mel Gibson.

"Wow! The best movie of all time!" he yelled with pure joy.

Tim and Lorna looked at each other, kind of resigned, but still smiling.

"Okay, we're gonna let you watch this, son." Tim laid his hand on Charlie's shoulder. "But don't forget to wake up early in the morning."

Charlie didn't look up at once. As his parents were on their way out he turned to them. "Sure, Dad," he said. "I'll take Kathy to school."

His parents turned to him, smiling with pride. "That's my boy," Tim said.

"Good night, Dad," Charlie said. "Good night, Mom."

"Good night, son."

"See you tomorrow," Lorna said.

They walked out.

*

The next morning saw Charlie still sitting in the couch, sleeping and snoring. Lorna walked in, already dressed and ready to go to work, as the banker that she was. She smiled as she saw him.

11

She walked to him and softly woke him up. "Hey Rambo, stop sawing wood," she said.

Charlie took his head between his hands, yawned it off, then he shook it violently.

"How was the film?" she asked. "Pretty boring, I suppose."

"I fell asleep right after it."

"Sure, sure. And the video game console, what's it doing in here?"

"Well…" Charlie said, showing embarrassment.

"C'me on, don't let your dad see you like this. And don't forget your little sister." She took the remote control and turned off the TV.

"I won't, Mom, I won't." Lorna saw an almost empty bottle on the floor, she picked it up. "Look, I only had a few mouthfuls, okay?" Charlie said. "We started drinking from it last night."

"You mean you started drinking from it last night. I didn't touch it, and your dad drank from the other bottle."

"Oh please, Mom…"

"Don't 'please' me. Look, if you wanna make a good soldier you need to slow down on this, if not to stay away from it."

"Yes, Mom."

"Don't say this just to make me happy."

"I'm not."

"Good. Rambo was no drunk."

"You don't know about that, anyway Rambo is not for real."

"But he's your hero. Right?"

Charlie gave up.

"Now go clean up. Your sister needs you." She helped Charlie up. "Hey."

"I suppose you're going now to work…"

"That's right. So I probably won't see you again before you leave."

"I guess not."

"Well…"

They hugged each other.

"Don't forget…" she started.

"…to put the ignition key in the glove compartment," he finished.

"You smell."

"I smell like a soldier ready to fight and serve his country."

"You've never smelt like that before."

"Isn't it a good sign?"

"Attention!" Lorna suddenly ordered, and Charlie sprang to attention. "At ease." He stood at ease. "That's my boy."

They hugged each other again.

*

The car abruptly stopped, its tyres screeching like crazy, the driver frantically putting his foot down on the brake pedal, to avoid Charlie and his complete US Army suit – uniform and hat, and the star-spangled banner all over him (chest, sleeves, hat, pants, even shoes) –, who was crossing the street without even having looked around first. The driver vomited loud insults as he left, and Kathy, who was following with her doll face, blond hair and typical schoolgirl clothes, burst out laughing.

Both kids were heading to Kathy's school, hand in hand.

"You know", Kathy said, "I'll always think a young boy like you should go to school and get some education."

"Because for you I have no education?"

"No, I mean…"

"You mean watching commercials and music videos on TV? Is that education to you?"

"We don't do only that…"

"They just teach you how to do the same things you do at home. They teach you how and where to spend your money."

"Last Friday we saw a French commercial."

"A what?"

"A commercial from France."

"Where's that?"

"It's a country in Europe."

"Eu… Europe? What is this? Is that what you guys are taught about, that kind of phony shit?"

"It sounds phony to you because you don't know about it," Kathy said.

"People should be taught how to protect themselves and protect our nation."

"Protect against what? We've got all the power, the money and the weapons!"

Charlie frowned. "Who told you that?" he asked.

"I heard it on TV."

"Whatever," he said, shaking his head.

"Do you read?" Kathy asked.

14

"Read? What for?"

Kathy gave up. She changed the subject. "Charlie?" she said.

"Yes."

"What's a drill?" she asked.

"Oh please, not again."

"Why don't you tell me?"

"Okay. It's the military word for exercise."

"Exercise?"

"Not your kind of exercise. I mean, not the school kind. Mine is physical. Much more physical." He didn't say any more.

"Why don't you tell me more?"

"About what?"

"About what you do as a soldier."

"Can't you guess?"

"I don't wanna guess, I wanna know."

"Well… you're a girl and you're too little to know."

"You mean I'm too little to understand?"

"That's right. I'll tell you more when you're a bigger girl."

"I wanna know now!"

"You wanna know everything now!"

"That's the way I am."

"And that's what makes you a little pain in the ass!"

They laughed.

"Why d'you wanna know about that now anyway?" Charlie asked. "Why is it such an emergency?"

"Because they may send you somewhere any

time to fight, and we won't see you again before some long time."

"They won't send me anywhere to fight," Charlie said with certitude, "I'm too young."

"They don't care about that!"

Charlie kept silent for a short moment. "You could be right," he finally said.

"Please tell me more."

"Just watch films and documentaries on TV."

"I wanna hear from you."

"Okay…" he sighed, starting to tell her more.

He did it with some pride, in some need to show the usefulness of being a soldier at the age of 16.

Charlie had quit high school and joined the US Army three months earlier, voluntarily. Of course he'd done it without even suspecting he would be the youngest person to do so. He'd done it for a good first reason, after a failed terrorist attack on American soil, in California. He'd been so suddenly scared and concerned for the security of his beloved nation and fellow citizens that he'd decided to make a big change in his life. The day after he'd seen a commercial on TV, advertising the merits of being a soldier and making a difference for the United States of America. And he hadn't hesitated one more second. His parents had agreed right away – even if they hadn't hidden their surprise – and always encouraged him, especially Tim who was a chief fireman, taking huge personal risks every day to keep his fellow citizens safe, and who was keeping saying to his son that the fires he was paid for controlling, could be started only by people outside the United States, especially from the Middle East. Which was a lie, less innocent than he thought it would be.

Joining the US Army hadn't been easy of course, because of Charlie's very young age, but Tim had always been there to bring weight. After multiple physical and mental and moral and psychological tests the army had finally accepted Charlie as a soldier, about to serve for the security and strength of the United States of America.

As he was taking his sister to school and telling her about being a soldier and going through a drill, he was on his way to get back to the barracks he was sent to in the first place.

"So? How was it?" he asked after he finished explaining.

"I didn't get anything," Kathy said.

"Of course. I told you you wouldn't understand."

"You get confused when you come to explain things to people."

"I don't get confused. You're the one who's too young and… anyway, here we are."

They were in front of the school all right.

"Thanks, Charlie."

"If they send me somewhere to fight before the next time I'm supposed to get back, I'll send you a postcard."

"I can't wait for it."

"You're so silly."

They hugged each other, laughing.

"Be a good girl."

"I will."

They separated and she walked to the entrance gate. When she got there, she turned to Charlie and sent him a goodbye kiss. He sent it back to her and she started walking through the school yard.

II

Four days later Charlie was among his pals, washing himself, getting rid of the signs from a hard day. The shower room was large, with its cubicles against the walls, they were private, even if there were no doors. As Charlie was taking a shower inside one of them, some boys were in the middle of the room, wiping their bodies with their towels, chatting, laughing, joking noisily.

As Charlie got out of his half-private cubicle, still naked, using his towel to wipe his body, all the other boys suddenly froze as two of them ran into Charlie and grabbed him, holding him tight.

"Hey! What… what are you doing?" he said, flabbergasted. "Turn me l… turn me loose!"

"Easy, Charlie boy," one of the two boys said, "just relax."

The others started to sing Wagner's bridal chorus and two more boys showed up, coming towards Charlie. There was a girl between them, coming towards him as well, wearing a white wedding dress, playing a bride. Her face was partly hidden, hardly visible. They walked to him, slowly, stepping in rhythm with the song.

Charlie stared at the girl, quite surprised. He didn't say anything right away. The two boys and the girl arrived beside him as the other boys finished singing.

"What the hell is this?" Charlie said.

Behind them a voice started speaking. Charlie and the girl turned round and saw a teen priest, with only a black towel around his waist, holding some kind of a bible. He was almost laughing.

"Now look, this is not funny, all right?"

The priest started speaking:

"You, young boy, do you want to marry this girl, to love her, to cherish her, till death do you part?"

"Are you serious?"

Around him the boys whispered, laughing: 'Say yes!' 'Yes!' 'Come on, you pussy, say the right word!'

"Oh, knock it off…!" Charlie said loudly.

One of the boys around the girl said 'I do!' and they all laughed.

Then the priest spoke again:

"And you, young girl, do you want to marry this boy, to love him, to cherish him, till death do you part?"

She turned to Charlie. She could see his face – and more than that. "Er…" she began, hesitating.

"I do!" another boy said, imitating a female voice. They all laughed again, except Charlie, the girl and the 'priest'. Who finished:

"You're married! Kiss each other!"

"What is this shit?" Charlie shrieked. "Nobody said yes anyway!"

Somebody said 'Of course you did!', another joker added, 'Both of you!' and they laughed once more, some other boys around saying 'Go ahead!' 'Do it, moron!' 'Kiss her!'

"Kiss who?" Charlie asked.

The girl turned to him and showed him her face. She was a young girl, around 17 or 18. A beautiful teenager. Charlie looked at her, stunned. Obviously, he'd never seen her before.

"Who are you?" he asked.

"She's your wife, stupid!" a boy answered. His name was Jay, he was one of the guys who brought the girl in.

"I'm outta here."

They all booed Charlie as he walked away, 'Pussy!' 'Faggot!' then they burst out laughing.

*

"Can't you take a joke, young man?" Manny asked.

They were all having dinner, their uniforms on. At Charlie's table were three other boys he was getting along with pretty well. But Charlie was by far the youngest person in the place, so he was the first target for more or less funny jokes.

Now he was trying to cool down – only trying, since the other guys were not helping much.

"I can't take stupid jokes," Charlie said.

"You're too serious, kid," argued Bill, one of the

guys facing him. "I've always told you that. Let yourself go."

"You just said, he's just a kid," explained Jay, the one sitting on his left. "He's too young."

"No, he's been taking himself too seriously," said Manny, the other one facing him. "He's the big star on the base."

"Why didn't you pick up an older fellow of yours for that kind of shit?" Charlie asked. "Who was the chick anyway?"

"You heard that, boys?" Manny said. "The 'chick'!" He laughed with the two other boys.

"I don't see what's so funny."

"You're starting to learn, Charlie. The way you speak is improving. Who knows, you may even lose your virginity tonight." The two others guffawed with Manny.

"Ha ha ha. Who's she?"

"She may tell you tonight," Jay said.

"What are you talking about?"

"She may tell you tonight," Jay repeated.

"Why? Did you arrange some other stupid joke or what?"

"Okay," Manny said, "forget about it, kid."

"Where did you find her anyway?"

The others chuckled.

"I think he kind of likes her," Bill said.

"I hate her. She was part of it."

"How can you know? She didn't know anything about you."

"That's what I'm saying. Maybe she was just a

24

little whore you paid just to show up and play that bride."

"Don't be silly," Jay said. "Nobody paid her. We just asked her, she said yes."

"So you made fun of her too!"

Manny shook his head. "Okay wise kid," he said, "eat your meal and shut your mouth."

There was a moment of silence at the table.

"Next time you guys try to find something funnier," Charlie finally said, "that one really sucked."

"Just keep showing us you can eat something else than pussy," Manny retorted.

Him and the two others laughed out.

"Speak for yourself, nasty asshole," Charlie said.

*

Thirty minutes later Charlie got into his dorm room, alone. There were eight beds in the room, and four guys inside, Charlie included. The others' names were John, Rick and Donald.

"Hi, Charlie boy," one of them said.

"Hi," Charlie said.

None of them were part of those who 'organized' the little party in the shower room.

"It stinks in here," Charlie said, working on his closet.

"You're a fine one to talk," Rick said back. "You've been smelling for some time. You know that?"

"It stinks anyway."

"Oh, we're very sorry," John said. "We haven't taken showers yet."

"I heard that's the first step on your way to turn outlaw," Charlie said.

"No shit," Rick said. "You know very much, for a new-born."

"Billy the Kid used to never wash himself. He used to smell worse than a pig."

"But in spite of that he used to get laid every night. I guess you didn't know that."

"I guess I don't know that much."

"What about you, kid? How many times has the clean wise guy that you are, got laid?" Donald asked him.

"Do me a favour, forget about me."

"Oh come on, Charlie the Kid!" John moaned. "Don't let us down…"

Then a man entered the room. He was a sergeant. All the boys sprang to attention. The sergeant walked along the room, checking the cases and closets. Then he suddenly turned to Charlie, who couldn't hide his surprise.

"Private Bradshaw, don't you have anything to say about what happened in the shower room?" the sergeant asked him, in a hoarse voice.

"N… no, sir," Charlie managed to answer. He was expecting anything but this.

The sergeant insisted: "Nothing?"

"Nothing, sir."

"That girl was brought to this place without any legal authorization from us."

"I didn't know about this, sir."

"I suppose you don't. And that's the problem. If you don't have anything to do with this, then why didn't you come to us and report what happened?"

"I… I didn't think about it, sir."

"You didn't think."

"It was just a joke, sir. Nothing serious."

"What about if I tell you… that the girl is the daughter of one of your chiefs, what would you say?"

"I… I wouldn't know what to say, sir…"

"You don't know much, do you?"

"I don't know, sir."

John, Donald and Rick laughed under their breaths.

"She'd like to know more about the young moron who volunteered for the US Army at age 16. You may meet her again tonight. Outside. You walk away from her again and you'll volunteer some place else, you hear?"

"Yes, sir."

"What happened in the shower room was more serious than you think."

"Yes, sir."

"Right." The sergeant turned away from him and walked around the room, continuing to talk without looking at any of the guys. "Tonight you soldiers watch the weather forecasts on TV. There's a storm alert for the next two or three days. Maybe even tomorrow. But tomorrow's drill is still on, so don't forget to dress warm and thick. We need all of you guys. Have a good evening." As he walked to the exit: "At ease."

The boys stood at ease as he left.

"What's the matter with everybody tonight?" Charlie complained. "They're all on me…"

"Didn't you get it?" Donald replied, grinning. "There was a sex party planned in the shower room tonight, with you as the first guest. And you blew it all."

"What did you expect when you joined the army in the first place?" John said. "It's full of wackos!"

The three boys laughed out.

"Can't you see you don't belong here?" Rick said.

"Why?" said Charlie in a challenging tone. "Because I'm too stupid?"

"No! Because you're a baby!"

"There are only babies here. I'm the youngest one of all, that's all."

"That's not all," Donald said. "The young baby that you are shouldn't stay permanently surrounded by adult males, especially when they can go to war at any time. Period."

"Oh yeah? And why shouldn't he?"

"Because it could give him the worst idea about girls," Donald answered, chuckling.

"We've all just had the greatest evidence of it," Rick finished.

They laughed again.

"This is bullshit," Charlie said, shrugging.

"You should be at school," John said. "Get some education and meet plenty of girls."

"Have you ever been to school?"

"Of course!"

"What kind of question is that?" Rick said in a surprised tone.

"So what the hell are you doing here?" Charlie asked John.

"What do you think?" John said. "I failed to be educated enough for what I wanted to be. So I took another track. So did most of the other guys. It doesn't mean you are going to fail too. You still have your chance. And you're just wasting it."

"What d'you know about it? I'm not wasting nothing at all anyway. I've always wanted to be a soldier. I don't need to graduate with anything for that."

"That's what you think," Donald said.

"Actually you're all jealous of me because I didn't waste my time at school."

The three boys looked at each other, stunned.

"All right, forget it," Rick said finally. "After all we're not your parents or your chiefs. You do whatever you want."

"That's right," Charlie approved.

"While you're at it why don't you get out of this stinking room and go meet your next wife?" John suggested.

"She will wait. Especially after what just happened."

"I met my wife when I was only 14."

"At least nobody played some stupid joke on both of you. Nobody forced you to marry her then, either."

"Get outta here, you moron!" Rick said.

"Your next wife is right about that," John said.

"About what?" Charlie said. "What did she tell you?"

"You may find out tonight."

"And you mean *your* next wife. I'll leave her to you. I can bet you won't stay married for a long time anyway."

"You better watch your mouth."

"Anyway I'm too young to marry her or anybody else, you know that. And I certainly won't marry the daughter of one of those big shots out there. I'm here to become a soldier, not a gigolo under command."

"I see. So I guess you'll be almost happy if tomorrow our country is attacked," Rick said. "Right?"

"If it can make you happy to believe that crap…"

Another boy came in. His name was Leo. A 19-year-old soldier, Charlie's best friend at the base.

"Hey Charlie, are you going out tonight?" he asked.

"Sure," Charlie said, nodding. "I'm starting to choke in here."

He left the room with Leo.

Within the next two minutes they were at the game room, relaxing, surfing on the Internet, shopping a little, playing video games. Charlie was in front of a big screen, shooting at it with a machine gun, a toy of course. He was doing pretty good. He was even the best player at this game.

After a moment his toy ran empty, he ejected the

loader, replaced it with another one and started shooting at the screen again. Shooting at enemies of the country.

*

Charlie was now outside the base, in civilian clothes, so was Leo, walking on a sidewalk beside him. The sky was dark and cloudy, the weather a bit windy.

"Same place?" Charlie asked.

"Probably," Leo replied.

"Cool."

"What happened tonight?"

"Oh, just fellows who wanted me to get some taste of marriage."

Leo looked at him. "What?"

"They know I don't have a girlfriend, so they kind of believe I'll never get married. Something like that."

"But you're only 16!"

"And I'm in the army."

"No comment."

"Shit! I'm starving," Charlie said. "Let's try the bakery first."

They walked across the street and pushed a bakery's entrance door.

The next place they visited that night was a bar, both of them holding a small package from the bakery.

They walked to the counter. A pretty barmaid,

31

looking over 30, came to them. Leo picked up the 'menu' sheet.

"Hello kiddos," the barmaid started.

"Hello," Leo said.

"What's it gonna be, cuties?"

"The usual," Charlie said.

"Sure thing."

"I'll take another cocktail." Leo showed her something on the menu. "This one."

"Okay." She walked away. Soon she started working on the two cocktails, and as she did another beautiful barmaid, looking much younger, came to them.

"Good evening," she said.

"Hello," Leo answered.

"Hi," Charlie said.

"What do you need tonight?" she asked.

"We've already ordered."

"Oh, sure." She showed an embarrassed smile. "Sorry."

"No problem," Leo said.

"That's cool," Charlie confirmed.

The girl turned to Charlie and kind of stared at him. "Haven't we met somewhere, young man?" she asked him.

"Sure. Every evening, right here," he said.

"I mean somewhere else."

"Yeah? And where?"

"Where? Well… in some shower hall, inside the base… you know…"

Charlie almost leaped up. "What…"

"…for that fake marriage," she explained laboriously. "I'm the… you know, the 'Bride'."

"Yeah," Charlie nodded, with some despair.

"No shit, Charlie…" Leo was amazed too, of course, but he took this a lot different way. "What's your name?" he asked her.

Right at this moment the other barmaid showed up with the cocktails and laid them in front of the others. "You ain't off yet, baby," she said to her teenage partner.

"I know."

"Don't stay around here."

"Thank you," Charlie said to her.

But the young barmaid stuck to it: "I'm Veronica. You're Charlie, right?" she asked.

Charlie stared at her, not believing his ears. "Jesus," he said. "We don't even have to shake hands."

"Charlie!" Leo said, a bit shocked.

"Both of you, go take a table," Veronica said.

She turned away, going back to work. Charlie and Leo picked up their drinks, then they went to the closest free table and had their seats.

"What's the matter with you?" Leo said. "That chick is gorgeous!"

"I like the other one better," Charlie said innocently.

"Don't be silly, she's 34! She could be your mother!"

"I don't care."

They both guffawed.

After twenty seconds they looked up at the bar

33

counter. Veronica was continuing doing her job behind it, making cocktails, filling glasses with beer, wine, sodas or other beverages, water included.

Charlie and Leo were drinking their cocktails quite slowly. They were a bit too strong for them.

"So she'd be the daughter of some military hot shot around here," Charlie announced.

"Really?"

"I've been told that today. It was not a joke."

"So she's well-known among the guys."

"You bet she is. I've also been told twice that I might meet her again tonight. Bingo."

"You're well-known too," Leo reminded him. "Celebrities attract themselves, you know the deal."

They looked at the bar again.

"She's gone!" Leo said suddenly.

She really was. There were still two girls behind the bar, but none of them was Veronica. The older one was still there.

"Where is she?" Charlie said.

"Maybe she went to the bathroom."

"No. There's another girl working now."

Right at this moment Veronica showed up from one side right in front of them, holding a chair. "Hey guys!" She put the chair down and had a seat.

Charlie was speechless. Leo could say something: "But you were…"

"Yes, I just finished," she said. "It's 10 pm. I'm off."

"I see," Charlie said, checking his watch.

34

"Look Charlie," she said to him, "I know you're upset…"

"Good guess."

"Your friends told me you'd enjoy the joke."

"They're not my friends and they fooled you too."

"How could I know?" Veronica said. She was looking almost as upset as he was. Or was trying to.

"I'm not blaming you. I suppose they paid you?"

"Charlie, come on!" Leo said.

"Do you really need to know about that?" she said.

"Not really," Charlie answered, indifferently. "Congratulations, anyway."

"I can give you the money, if you like."

Charlie looked at her, a bit incredulous. "So they did pay you…"

"Yeah," she said, shrugging.

"They told me they didn't."

"What difference does it make?"

"None. You can give the dough back to those guys."

"I could," she said, trying to be provocative.

"You would?" Leo asked.

"I could."

"You could give it to me."

"In your dreams," she said.

"Whatever you want," Charlie said.

"I'll give it to you."

"Don't be silly, I don't want any of this. All I want is to be left alone."

"Oh, am I bothering you that much…?"

"It's not you," Charlie replied, "it's all this. All this shit. As you probably know, I joined the US Army three months ago. And things went pretty normal, you know, nice and cool… until the press showed up, last month. They wanted to know the new youngest guy ever incorporated as a committed volunteer. Since then, I can hardly live. It started with some bubblehead saying to me, 'Now you're in the Guinness Book, you can go home'. Then the stupid jokes came out, one after another, almost every day. Until this one, the ultimate one. The marriage. What's next? A fake terrorist attack? I'm tired of this shit. All those guys think they know what's the best for me, only because they're older. They don't know shit. I want to be left alone. As a committed US soldier. Nothing else."

They sat there for a short moment, as dumb as graves.

"Wow… that was deep, Charlie," she finally said. "Too bad you didn't bring a loud-speaker. No offence."

"I want to serve the United States of America. Our country has a lot of enemies and needs to be protected. Would you rely on an old creep pushing buttons behind his desk to do that?"

"I guess not," she said.

"When I reach the age of 21, I will be treated like a real soldier. But until then I'll have to take their bull. D'you think it's normal?" he asked with much annoyance.

"No, Charlie. But that's the way it is. Take the

positive out of all this shit. It'll be making you stronger, and tougher."

"Yeah. And what will I look like when I'm 21? A block of granite?"

"Charlie, calm down. You're not very smart…"

"What's making you smarter than I am?"

"…but I still like you very much. You got heart and guts."

"Huh…? I got heart and guts now? What's making you say that?"

"You know what. You just told about it. You need heart and guts to get incorporated that young. Voluntarily."

"Oh… if you say so. You know what? You're sounding just like my mother."

"And you won't look like a block of granite at 21," she continued, ignoring the argument, "first because you'll have struck those guys back, way before that."

"Second?"

She smiled. "Second… well, because you may get married way before that too."

"Wow. Are you some astrologist or what?"

"I'm planning to be."

"No joke? How old are you?"

"I'm 17. Just like you."

"I'm 16."

Charlie, Leo and Veronica walked out of the bar. They were welcome by the wind, which had become a bit stronger than it was before.

"Well, see you, Veronica," Charlie said. "Have a good night."

"Where are you guys going?" she asked innocently.

"We're going back, lady," Leo said. "It's 10.45."

"Do you want to?"

"You know we have to," Charlie said.

"You know who I am, Charlie. I can say something about it. What d'you think?"

*

The next morning a non-commissioned officer walked in Charlie's dorm room, switching on the lights.

"Wake up guys! Wake up, come on!" He walked across the room, checking the guys, making sure they would wake up and get ready to get off their beds and stand up.

John called for him. "Sir?" he said.

The non-com stopped by his bed. "Yeah?"

"Is Bradshaw here?" John couldn't see Charlie's bed from the one he was lying in.

The non-com turned his head to Charlie's bed, then back to John. "I guess not," he said.

Charlie's bed was empty. And perfectly untouched.

"Where is he?" John asked.

"Not your business, soldier." The non-com left, adding nothing more.

John got up. "Son of a bitch..." he said, smiling

with some envy. "You'll see pals, he'll never say thank you for this."

He'd never understand how right he was.

Outside the wind was rather strong.

III

During the exercise, the wind was blowing hard enough so the guys were spending most of the time on the ground, or fighting to keep their balance. Every time they lost it and fell down, they got yelled at by the closest officer, who himself had much difficulty to keep his own balance.

Crawling, running, climbing, jumping… and fighting something they couldn't see but could feel: the wind. The guys were feeling it hard on their bodies, especially of course when they had to run against it. This was when things were turning the hardest way. And when the officers were yelling the loudest.

"Come on, babies!" one of them was barking. "Come on, you worthless worms! Push on your legs! Who sent you here, the Salvation Army? Come on, you virgins, go faster! Make enemies of your poor, lousy selves! More important, make an enemy of the wind! Imagine it's Russian, or German, or Japanese, or Arabian! Or even Canadian, or French!"

Charlie was one of the guys running against the wind – and fighting hard to move forward – when he heard this. "French..." he whispered.

The officer was struggling to keep his balance while watching – and while yelling through the wind instead of facing it. "Now fight, guys! I want you to fight! To fight, you hear me?"

They didn't move any faster.

"You hear me?" he continued. "You think this wind is natural? You think it's been brought to us by your God? By our God? You're fuckin' wrong! You're damn fuckin' wrong, 'cause it's not! It's the work of our enemy! Or of two of 'em! Or maybe from all of them, put together! All allied against us, right at this moment! Imagine this is World War III! The United States of America against the Rest of the World!"

"That's right! World War III!" Charlie yelled back. But his voice was still partly covered by the wind, so the officer hardly heard it.

"Now what are you waiting for?" the officer howled. "The enemy is trying to push you back, to make you weaker and weaker, he's about to crush you, he's about to tear you apart, what are you gonna do? Let him do that without any resistance from you guys?!"

"No, no...!" Charlie shrieked.

"I'll tell you what you're gonna do! You're gonna fight the wind, you're gonna fight the enemy, again and again and again, and you'll push him away, always stronger and stronger, in the end you won't even feel it any more! And you will win!"

"*Yeah!*"

This was loud enough to be heard by everybody around. "Shut up, jerk!" somebody said, but nobody heard.

"Now keep running!" the officer yelled. "Faster than that! Go, go, go, go, go!"

The guys kept running, as fast as they could. As they did, the wind kept blowing harder and harder.

*

In the end the wind was too powerful, so the drill had to be stopped. And the warning to be given. And the base to be upside down.

There was the noise of the siren. The alert siren.

The soldiers were now running all across the buildings and the main yard. This time there was no more time for discipline. But they were all converging to the same points: the exit, then the cars and jeeps parked outside the base.

It was very dark. The sky had turned to gray black almost in one moment, covered with the heaviest clouds that could exist.

There was a storm. And at one point of the sky, emerging from the clouds down to the earth… there was something.

Some of the guys were packing their stuff. This was part of another kind of exercise that had been given to them: evacuate the place, as fast as they could. They could hear more or less panicked voices shrieking from the swarmed corridors; yelling things like: "Come on, come on, go, go, go, go, go…!"

Some other guys had not started to pack. One of the rooms could witness three of them; two were stuck at the window, watching with disbelief.

"Jesus Christ…" one of them said.

"I'll be damned…" the other one whispered.

Soon they were joined by the third one. "What's that?" he asked.

They had a quick glance at him, saying nothing.

The thing was coming to the barracks, fast. It was a twisted column of air, rotating very quickly, like a top. It just didn't stop. And it was much bigger. And so much more violent. Even from the window they could see it destroying everything on its way.

A tornado.

With thunder and lightning breaking out all around it, especially on its top, acting like its deputies.

The three guys were brutally grabbed from behind and taken away from the windows by two big-looking newcomers, in fact sergeants who forced them to pack up, and fast.

Charlie was still in his dorm room, alone and still packing up! Of course he was doing it in a hurry, but he had too much stuff to put into his bags.

A soldier appeared in the room. He saw Charlie and his eyes widened. "What the hell are you still doing here?" he asked, flabbergasted. "D'you wanna die or what? Move your ass out of here!"

But he didn't make Charlie do it. He just left the room quickly.

Charlie kept packing, but after a moment he gave up. He closed his three bags and started out, leaving some of his stuff behind. No more time.

He was only on his way out when the building started shaking, vibrating. All the lights went off. Soon the noise became unbearable.

Just after Charlie managed to leave the room, a window exploded. Then another. The beds and closets started moving across the room, soon one then two of the closets were tossed down. More followed.

Once in the dark corridor he was hit from behind by something and collapsed. He stood back up and started running to one of the ends of the building, then he went down the stairs to the exit door. It was the closest one to the gate.

Once he got outside Charlie lost his balance and was thrown straight down, across the stairs to the ground.

The wind was blowing like crazy, so hard that it was whistling. Charlie stood up, picked up his bags and looked up. Now the tornado was quite close to the barracks, about to erase it from the surface of the earth. Some pieces of the buildings torn apart by it were already flying across the yard. The soldiers had to dodge them while running to the gate.

At this sight Charlie just couldn't move. He only stood there, watching with round eyes. For a split second he thought that the world was coming to an end, that this cyclone was about to destroy it, and his beloved country along with it.

A soldier running by saw him. He came to him, then he shook him like an apple tree, yelling: "Come on, stupid! You wanna get wasted or what?" He started to drag Charlie as fast as he could, taking him to the open gate. Charlie showed absolutely no reaction, not even aware that somebody was 'piloting' him. "Help me!" the soldier was yelling at him. "Help me, dammit!"

Charlie kind of woke up. He finally saw the soldier; then he looked down and saw something, a machine gun attached to his belt. He took it, then he turned loose, dropping his bags.

"Hey! What the f…" The soldier couldn't believe his eyes.

"This is it!" Charlie shrieked. "The enemy!" And he ran away… *to the tornado itself.*

"Come back here!" the soldier yelled.

Charlie didn't come back. He kept running.

The tornado reached the barracks, starting to tear everything apart on one side. Charlie was violently pushed aside but this didn't prevent him from starting to… shoot at it.

The machine gun was real and loaded with real bullets.

The soldier joined him and grabbed him hard from behind. "Cut that shit out, you fuckin' idiot, move it!" The noise was forcing him to scream like he never did before.

He started to drag him back to the gate but Charlie was fighting to turn loose.

"No! We gotta push it back!" Charlie yelled.

"What the fuck are you talking about? Come on!"

"*No!!* We can win! We have to win!"

The soldier grabbed a post and tried to use it to drag Charlie back more. But Charlie turned again, and started shooting again at the tornado.

"This is my country!" he screamed, as he was firing. "Get out of here! Out of my country!"

"*Get back!!*"

Outside the gate the other soldiers were screaming too. Some of them had got off the trucks.

"*You can't win!!*" Charlie yelled at the tornado.

The building in front of Charlie started to break and blow up under the force and Charlie himself started to lose it, his mind as well as his body. He was not heavy enough so he started to get lifted off the ground.

The soldiers at the gate were screaming at Charlie to get back but he didn't hear them. He still wasn't really aware of anything around him and the noise was too loud.

The other soldier was lifted off the ground too, and he had to release Charlie in order to have a better grab on the post, with his two hands, and to stay grounded. Charlie started to panic, and he stopped firing, trying to use something to hold on and he was finally lifted off the ground for good, screaming but shooting again at the tornado as it was sucking him in.

The other soldier was holding on, grabbing the post as tight as he could, but the tornado was coming closer and closer. Then something landed under him. "Catch it!" two other soldiers yelled. It was a fire-hose nozzle. The soldier managed to pick it up and the other guys started pulling. He released the post and was finally taken back to the gate, then they all ran to the trucks which rolled away at once, as the tornado was destroying the barracks, very progressively, wiping out everything on its way.

*

As it kept moving across the barracks, pulverizing every building on its way, Charlie kept spinning around inside the tornado, at high speed, shooting and shrieking things like: "*You don't have the right!!*"

Soon the machine gun ran empty and he threw it away, furious. The gun started to spin around with him.

He was pretty lucky because as he was keeping turning around and around he was also moving up, dodging the buildings and their pieces without even knowing. He always went up and up, very progressively, getting sucked up to the source of the tornado, at the top. Irresistibly dragged. While lightning was breaking through.

As he was going up there was always more lightning breaking in from the black, furious clouds, tearing the tornado apart, opening black holes that closed all by themselves almost immediately. And as he was still dragged to the top and reached that zone, Charlie was suddenly hit at point blank by one of those electric discharges and he disappeared, just like that. Disintegrated.

His first trip had just begun.

The tornado didn't care, it just kept going, rotating and destroying.

Part

TWO

Twenty-one years later.

A beautiful young girl in a white bikini, wearing sunglasses, was busy getting as tan as possible, on the deck of a small yacht off San Francisco. Everything about and around her was showing it was summer. The sea was quiet, the weather was good. There was only one large, dark cloud in the sky.

The girl was alone on the deck, lying on a folding chair, on her back. At one moment there was lightning tearing the cloud apart, moving across it, then down to the sea. And something appeared, sort of released, falling down; she couldn't see it, but she could hear it falling into the sea with a big splash.

She frowned, took her sunglasses off, then she half stood up on her chair and started looking around. And she saw that the water had become rough, in the distance, not that far from the boat.

She stood up, went to the railing and watched the water.

"Dan!" she called. No response came so she called again, louder: "*Dan!!*"

"What?" a male voice said, from inside the boat.

"Come on out!"

"Why? Not enough sun?"

"Just come out here!"

Soon the boy called Dan showed up. He was young of course, and half naked.

The girl pointed at the water. "Something just fell down," she said. "Look!"

"I don't see anything," Dan said.

"Of course you don't see anything, it's under water now! Look at the water! It has changed!"

"It looks pretty quiet to me," Dan said, shrugging.

"I heard something falling down in the water," she objected.

"What was it?"

"I don't know, I didn't see it. I only heard it."

"In some dream."

"I wasn't dreaming, you idiot!"

"That thing would have fallen down from where?"

"I don't know."

"Maybe jokers who cast something out."

"Yeah, tell me where they are? All I can tell you, I heard a noise, and I saw the water, it had changed."

"What can I tell you?"

She didn't say anything more so he went back inside the boat. She stood there for a short moment, watching. Nothing happened.

After ten seconds she shrugged and got back on her folding chair, putting her sunglasses back on.

*

A few hours later, the sun was going down on the sea. The big cloud was gone, leaving the darkening sky as clear as the water. The beach was not deserted, far from it. There were still many people enjoying the good weather, lying down on the sand or playing on the shore.

Among them was a couple, running along the shore, close to the water and waves. Two young people, both white. The woman was Laura Parker Ingrams, a 36-year-old brunette, a former athlete who'd never won anything through competitions and who'd retired quickly after she got married. She was slim and beautiful in her special way. The man was Stuart Dano. A blond-haired playboy, 33, with nothing much to him but his playboy style. They were having their evening jog, in silence.

It was getting dark and they couldn't see everything on the wet sand.

After a moment Laura suddenly tripped over something and fell down, face forward.

Stuart didn't notice right away and kept running ahead. Until Laura called. "Hey!"

Stuart heard it and looked on his right side. Nobody, no more woman running beside him.

He stopped running and looked behind him. She was standing back up, catching her breath. He ran back to her.

"What's the matter?" he asked, disconcerted. "Are you okay?"

"Yeah." All her front body and clothes were covered with wet sand, her face included.

"What happened?"

"I fell," she said.

"You fell? How could you fall?"

"Dunno. Stumbled over something." She was still breathing quickly, heavily, wiping the sand off her face. "Give me a moment."

"Sure. But... stumbled over what?"

"How the hell can I know...? Let me breathe, for Christ's sake!" Instinctively she had a look back, at what made her fall. So did he.

And they saw it.

"What's that?" Laura asked.

"It looks like..."

A human body. In a green US Army uniform. All soaked. Rejected by the sea. Laura leant toward it and turned it over.

"My God!" She was so shocked that she had to catch her breath more. She managed to kneel close to the body.

"It's a kid!" Stuart said, amazed.

Unconscious. She used her hand to clear the kid's face. "A little boy," she said. "Jesus, a little boy!"

"A little soldier..."

She checked the boy's heart, then his pulse. "He's alive!" she almost screamed.

Stuart couldn't believe this. "No kidding?"

"Call an ambulance. Now!" she ordered.

"I don't have my cell phone on me," he said. "Neither do you I guess. I left mine in your car."

"Then tell somebody around to! Can't you see this is urgent?"

He ran away. In the meanwhile Laura tried to bring the boy back to consciousness, by all means available and necessary... impossible.

Stuart managed to make an old lady call an ambulance, and soon a growing bunch of people converged to the scene, as a pair of patrol men noticed what was going on and ran to it.

*

Soon the boy was lying on a bed, in a hospital room. Still unconscious of course. Looking in a deep coma. He was hardly breathing. For the moment there was nobody but him in the room. The light was very bright inside.

Laura and Stuart were sitting on chairs, outside the room, against one of the walls. Waiting for fresh news. Not the kind of news expected from doctors. Some photographers were standing around the closed room door. They were not allowed to get in the room and some police officers were also standing in the corridor, watching them close.

Soon two people showed up, walking to Laura and Stuart. A man in a white coat and another man in civilian clothes. The civilian produced something looking like a police badge. "My name is Jim

Robredon," he announced. "From the San Francisco Police Department."

"So?" Laura said, indifferent. Enough not to shake hands with him. Neither did Stuart. "You're a cop?" he asked.

"Detective, to be more specific."

"And you are?" Stuart asked the other man.

"I'm a doctor," the man said.

"No, I mean, what's your name?"

"Sanford."

"What's with the boy?" Laura asked him.

Robredon interrupted, being faster to the doc. "First of all, are you relatives?" he asked.

"You mean, the two of us and the boy?" Laura asked back.

"Yes."

"No, absolutely not," she answered, shaking her head. "We haven't even met. Just found him unconscious on the beach. That's all."

"How did you get to find him?"

"Well," Stuart said, "we were jogging together on the beach, along the shore, and..."

"...I stumbled over him and fell down," she continued. "Of course I didn't know it was a human body... It could have been anything else, a piece of wood or something... I turned to look and... you can guess what's next."

"You guys found him close to the water, right?" Robredon questioned.

"Yeah... as a matter of fact he was in the water," Stuart said.

"That's right," Laura approved, nodding. "I

would have seen the body if it was lying anywhere else. The waves didn't make it clearly visible."

"Do you have any idea about what the boy was doing there, how he could have ended up in… you know…"

"Again detective, we only found him," Laura said. "That's all. The rest has nothing to do with us."

"We don't know anything about that kid," Stuart added.

"Neither do we," Robredon said.

"What do you mean?" Laura asked.

"I mean we don't know anything about this boy either," Robredon said. "Who he is, where he came from, nothing. We didn't find any ID on him. His face is not in our file of missing persons and believe me, we've checked carefully. We also took his fingerprints, we put them in every file we have, our criminal one included, and we didn't find anything. Nobody's looking for him, in any way. He ain't searched or wanted anywhere."

Laura turned to Sanford after a silent moment. "How is he doing, doctor?"

"Well, he's okay, we've checked his whole body except his brain, we've also checked his blood and haven't found anything unusual. He's in perfect condition."

"So why is he in a coma?" she asked.

"I don't know," the doc said, shaking his head with perplexity. "We haven't scanned his brain yet. We can't do that as long as he's in a coma, without an authorization from a parent of his."

"What was he doing in the water anyway?" Robredon said, speaking to himself more than to the others.

"How did he survive the sea?" the doc added, the same way.

"How long has he been under water? Was he really in the water?" Robredon continued. "Maybe somebody dropped him on the sand and left. We can't neglect any possibility. We may be dealing with an unwanted child."

"I don't know," Laura said, unconvinced. "He's too big for that. Babies are usually unwanted."

"Usually, but not always," Robredon objected.

"If he's such a case, he should appear in your file within the next few days," Stuart said.

"Yes, unless he's from another state." Then, suddenly: "D'you both have kids?" Robredon asked.

"What kind of question is that?" Stuart said.

"Just answer it."

"I don't have any," Laura said.

"You mean personally?"

"Yeah, personally."

"You?" Robredon asked Stuart.

"Me neither. Why?"

"Are both of you guys married?"

"No!" Laura said loudly. "Why, should we be?"

"Just asking."

Laura had a quick glance at Stuart, who didn't say anything. Then: "I am married, but not to him." She showed her ring.

"You're married?" Robredon asked Stuart, who

answered with another question: "What's the connection with the boy?"

"Are you married?" Robredon asked again.

"No, I'm not."

"Who are you to her?"

"What's this?" Laura said, a little annoyed. "Are you a cop, or a marriage counsellor?"

"Okay, the point is," Robredon explained, "since the boy is still unwanted and you're the one who found him, you have the possibility to keep him with you."

"From your mouth, it sounds like a serious case."

"I'm concerned in a way. And to be honest with you, I don't have any kids either."

"Neither do I," the doctor said.

"I'm still single," Robredon added.

"I'm married," Sanford specified, "but my wife can't have any kids."

"I guess everybody could be on a possible wanting list, and you guys would be on top. Especially you," Robredon said to Laura, "since you're married."

"My husband doesn't want any kids," Laura said.

"Do you?" Robredon asked.

"I do…"

"That's what really matters here, I guess."

"But it's still up to the boy and what he will say when he wakes up, right?" Laura said.

"Right… Problem is, as long as he doesn't say anything, people will talk about him. Tomorrow he'll probably make the headlines."

"Why would he?"

"There's been people saying that they didn't notice the boy lying on the sand until you did."

"This is normal, I didn't notice the body myself until I stumbled over it," Laura said.

"It sort of fits something else. There's also a young girl claiming that the boy has fallen down into the sea from the sky."

"Oh, really?" Laura chuckled along with them.

"It's on TV."

The girl Robredon was talking about was the same one lying on that little yacht off the city when she heard something (or somebody) falling down from nowhere into the water. After the boy was discovered she'd called the press, almost immediately. "I was on a boat when I heard the sound of something falling in the water," she said in front of the microphones and flashing cameras. She was still wearing her sunglasses. "A big *splash,* you know. This occurred behind me so I didn't see anything, I only heard it. And now they've been talking about that unknown little boy who was found on our shore and I can't help thinking that…"

"Her boyfriend," Robredon continued, "told the press not to take her seriously, that she's just trying to attract attention to herself. I guess he still is. So there is this, and also the fact that the boy was dressed as a US Army soldier. He was wearing the uniform for committed volunteers."

"Really?" Laura said.

"Yes, really."

"He's a kid!"

"You don't know how old he is. Anyway they think he can be identified from that lead. Some army officials have already dropped by here to take his fingerprints. That's two reasons among others."

*

The morning after. Some newspapers were spread across a table, with somebody picking them up one after another. A man, named Paul Ingrams, 41. Laura's husband. A rich, handsome, caring citizen – he was also ready to help kids even though he didn't like them very much. He was alone in the house, standing by the table. Dressed up as the businessman that he really was. He was running a big automobile firm as well as a foundation – so he was very busy. Laura was not there.

Almost all the newspapers' headlines were about that little boy found by much chance on the beach the day before.

He took out a cell phone from one of his pockets and dialled his wife's phone number.

Laura and Stuart were in her car, Laura behind the wheel. There was a ring, she took a minuscule mobile phone out.

She recognized her husband's number and didn't take the call.

"It's him again?" he asked.

"Yeah." She let the ringing continue until it stopped and the voicemail took over.

Paul sighed with frustration. He put his cell phone away and left the room.

Laura made her device disappear. She had spent the whole night in and out of the hospital. She didn't know why and wasn't trying to ask herself. Was she trying to protect the kid? She didn't want to know. Stuart, who'd had nothing better to do, had stayed with her.

"Why didn't you take it?" Stuart said.

"He knows I'm here," she said. "I don't wanna talk to him about it. Nothing's stopping him from coming over here."

"So he sees you with me?"

"Nothing's stopping you from going."

"What difference does it make, if I go or not? He knows about us now, no matter what the cop said to the press. He's not stupid."

"He can read."

"He can spy on people, too. He's the big man."

"What d'ya mean by that? That he knew about us way before last night?"

"You're his wife, you ask him," he said back.

"Okay," she said softly, with a nod.

"Don't get me wrong, I don't resent you in any way."

"Sure you don't."

"Aren't you wondering why he didn't show up once in the whole night?"

"He's always busy," she only said.

"Even when he's asleep?"

"I'll take you home," she said, turning the ignition key and starting the engine. "There are too many press people outside."

"Okay, thanks." He looked at her. "What are you gonna do?"

"I'm gonna follow your advice. Ask him about us."

"Cool," he said ironically, maybe believing she didn't mean it.

She started the car. An electric one. The kind of car her husband was dealing with, through his automobile firm. The car peeled out of the parking lot and rolled away. Without making any noise. Or almost. (Now Paul was working on a new car prototype, still electric, able to rise off the ground and move around in the air. Such a car could be an answer and solution to traffic jams.) This was one of the notable changes made through the years, the internal combustion engine being replaced with special engines running on electricity or solar energy. All cars, buses and tramways were working now this same way, like metropolitan, underground subways all over the world were already doing way before. The result was that the air pollution had been halved, and there was almost no more sound pollution from working engines, except during road works. But that was almost all. The big polluting factories were still around, and of course technology had even more grown and increased, making everything always smaller – except the flat screen

TV sets. People could get all the satellite and cable TV channels on minuscule, highly sophisticated mobile phones, for instance. The DVDs, Blu-Rays and CDs were looking like chips. And there were TV commercials all over, shown on every hi-tech building façade and at almost every street corner. The TV image had invaded everything. More than ever. So well that paper books had faded away, they almost didn't exist any more. People needed a computer to be able to read a book, and when they were not home they were reading them using the smallest laptops they could find, or the gPad or iPad tablets, as well as all kinds of smartphones and reading devices such as Kindle or Nook, which became widespread. There were no more book-shops. And libraries and even street kiosks were on their ways to extinction.

The all digital had become the custom. Including in the deepest Midwest. Downtown San Francisco was shining brilliantly. The spotless frontages of its most sparkling glass skyscrapers, were now used as windows as well as as screens, as giant advertising panels, showing all the possible and conceivable messages. Among the multiple satellite dishes which had pride of places on top of the buildings, some were also used as projectors, which sent their images on the frontages that faced them. Some others of those satellite dishes, set on top of street lights, were projecting those images onto the glass frontages on the other side of the street. It was now this way in most of the largest American downtown areas, or at least in their wealthiest and most popular business districts, a real advertising festival, a permanent fair of images that reached its highest dimension after sunset. The people, wealthy or not, were enjoying the show all the more since it was free of charge. Or almost.

"Has anybody showed up anyway?" Stuart asked.

"Nobody came for the kid."

"What do you think of it?"

"Nothing yet."

"What about those religious people?"

"They don't count."

"You're conversational this morning," he said.

"What do you want me to say, after a sleepless night?" She turned her radio on and hit the news, which soon came to the mystery boy.

The same radio station was heard inside another car, a luxurious one driven by Paul. He was also sticking to those radio news, finally hearing nothing new or special about the young newcomer from the sea. So he turned off the radio and used his cell phone, dialling the number of one of his secretaries.

"Hello, Anita?" he said. "Look, I won't be there on time, all right? I'm on my way to the hospital, I don't know how long I'll stay there. But you'll see me today, and the others will as well, okay?"

"Are you on your way to visit *him*?" Anita's voice asked.

"Yes, I'm going to see that boy. I still haven't seen him. Since Laura found him she hasn't said a word to me. She's spent the whole night at the hospital and she didn't take any of my calls. I want to know what's with that kid is making my wife become like this. I'd just like you to spread the word. That I probably won't be there this morning. Thanks. See you later, Anita." He hung up.

He arrived at the hospital and found a way to park his car. As Laura said, there were many press people there. Without seeming to care much about them, he parked his car, got out of it and walked to the main entrance.

Very quickly surrounded by a bunch of journalists and photographers. Who pushed him around as they asked him a thousand questions at the same time.

A journalist with one of the strongest voices asked this one: "Your wife was with another man when she found that little boy. D'ya think he nails her while you give out your money so generously?"

Of course Paul heard this, as well as he heard the roar of laughter that followed. He stopped and turned his head to where the question came from but he couldn't spot the insolent guy. His eyes were like daggers. "Another question like that and I'll call my army friends so they wipe you out with their stuff," he said roughly. "My wife has the right to see whoever she wants."

He started walking again, the crowd roared again as it was moving with him. He ignored them, about to reach the steps leading to the entrance. Then... he was stopped by some other people, standing by the steps.

A young woman with protruding eyes and long white hair, walked out of the small group and came straight to him. "Mister Paul Ingrams?" she said.

"Yeah…" He was a little afraid.

"We'll pray for you… and for your wife," she said slowly.

"Good for you." He wanted to break through but the woman stood in his way, right in front of him. Nobody among the press people tried to stop her. They only kept using their camcorders and cameras, recording the scene, taking photos.

"You pray for her too, sir!" she added, louder. "Your wife is a sinner! She needs to repent, for the sake of the boy inside…"

"Let me pass, please."

Somebody else among the religious stepped forward. A man with a thick moustache. "Judgement Day is nigh, mister," he announced. "That boy inside has been sent to judge us."

"The Lord is back, sir," the white-haired woman concluded, before screaming, all of a sudden: *"He's back!! Back among us!"*

"Yes!!" the small group barked, then they started cheering noisily.

The woman turned back to Paul. "He needs to carry his cross so he can command us all and deliver…"

Paul broke through, interrupting her, followed by the whole press. Still, the voices kept following him: "Judgement Day!" "Hallelujah!"

He finally entered the hospital, with a big sigh.

The staff inside didn't let the press in. Paul was on his own again.

He walked to the reception desk. There was a woman behind.

"I'm Paul Ingrams," he announced.

"Oh…"

"Is my wife here?"

"Didn't you see her outside?" she asked.

"No… no."

"She's not here," she said. "Neither is the man who was with her."

"I see."

"We couldn't keep her in here, you know. She's not connected to that kid."

"She's still the one who found him."

"That's not enough for us to keep her here all night."

"Of course. I understand. I've never wanted you guys to do that." After a short pause. "I'd like to see the boy."

"Sure. Just a minute please. I need to tell the head office." She picked up the phone and pushed only one button. "Hello… oh, yes. Okay." She hung up, then, to Paul: "They saw you, of course. The room number is… 368. Fourth floor."

"Thank you."

"You can use the elevator."

"I will. Thanks again." He walked away. As he was walking to the elevator he noticed people standing or sitting all over the hall, reading the Bible, or Quran, or Torah, and mumbling. Some

Muslims were on their knees, their eyes closed. Some of the others looked up at him.

He pushed the button, waited for the elevator, then he got inside.

Doctor Sanford was already in the room when Paul showed up. Paul looked at the boy, still in his coma, then at the doctor. "So there's nothing wrong with him, right?" he asked.

"As far as I know, yes, nothing," the doctor said. "Basically, he could wake up at any moment. It depends on him only. Him and what's happening inside."

"Inside?"

"You know what I mean."

"Not really, no."

"Well, the cause of the coma is not a physical or blood problem. So I don't know what's going on, but something is."

Paul remained silent for a moment, trying to digest this. "All right."

"He could emerge now as well as in one year or two. If not more," the doctor continued. "We can't tell."

Paul nodded. He couldn't argue about this new fact. "So he doesn't need to be cared for in this hospital, right?" he said.

"Sorry?"

"You just said there was nothing wrong with him, with his blood and body…"

"Yes, but we still need to examine his brain. As

we already told your wife, we can't do that without an authorization from a parent of his."

"So the brain may be the problem?"

"If a problem there is."

"And nobody showed…"

"Nobody claimed to be his family so far."

"All right. Now listen," Paul took a deep breath. "I'll take him with me," he said.

The doctor opened wide, stunned eyes. "Sorry?" he said again.

"He's in perfect health, as far as you know, right?"

"Yes, but…"

"If there's nothing seriously wrong with him, if there's nothing you have to worry about, if he doesn't need any medical care, it would be better for him to wake up in a house than in a hospital," Paul said. "Yes or no?"

The doctor shrugged. "I suppose so, yes…"

"I'll assume total responsibility. If I end up with a mentally sick little creep in my hands, I'll assume it too."

"And what will you do?"

"I'll need to talk this over with my wife."

"You don't know anything about that kid," the doctor argued.

"You don't either. Nobody does. What difference does it make? Do we know anything about a newborn child either?"

"There's nothing to know about a new born child. There is about," the doctor nodded to the boy, "a teenager like him."

"The info will come," Paul said.

"All right. Your responsibility, anyway. I suppose you'll have to fill out some forms and stuff."

"No problem," Paul said, shrugging in his turn. "Even my wallet is open."

Right at this moment Laura came in the room.

"Wow," the doctor said, surprised. "A real family picture we got here."

"Can a doctor talk like that?" Laura asked.

"We're taking the kid with us," Paul said, going straight to the point.

"*What?*" she almost barked, opening her eyes wide in her turn.

"Oh… didn't you know?" the doctor asked her.

"I just made the decision," Paul explained him. He turned to her. "Don't tell me you're feeling sorry."

"I'm not feeling sorry…" she said, disconcerted.

"Good."

"Where are we…?" she started to ask.

"Not here." Paul turned to Sanford. "How can we do that without being noticed?"

"You might get yourselves and the whole hospital in trouble by doing this…"

"Come on, this kid is not supposed to stay here for ever. If needed I will pay."

"What about his brain?" Laura asked.

"If there was something wrong with it the kid would probably be awake by now, giving us his traumas. If I were you I'd worry about those lunatics outside. Did you notice them?" Paul asked her.

73

"I saw them all night long," Laura said.

"They already believe he's some Jesus Christ back on earth or whatever. I read some papers before I came and I saw a lot of rubbish, like that he'd been born from a whale, the reason why he was found lying on the beach. The longer he stays here, the more crazies will show up and the more he'll be at risk. We can't let that happen."

"We can have him transferred to a room on the first floor, then it's up to you," the doctor said before leaving the room.

Paul and Laura looked at each other, then Laura left the room too.

An hour later the boy, still in his coma, was lying on a mattress in another room, on the ground floor of the hospital. Laura had parked her car just in front of the window, with its back door wide open, ready to welcome him in.

Paul and the doctor gave the boy, still on his mattress, to Laura who was inside the car. She managed to take him in and laid him on the back seat, as best as she could.

As they were working on this they could hear voices of people singing 'Hallelujah', 'Hallelujah'… and canticles to the glory of God and His son back on earth.

Laura shut the car's back door, then she took the driver's seat and drove away. Without the car making any noise (or almost), and without any of the press and religious people noticing anything.

Paul watched Laura driving away, then he pulled back and left the room, followed by the doctor.

He left the hospital through the entrance door. He did this on purpose, to be noticed by everybody outside. The reporters rushed to him, being faster than the religious, he walked through without answering any question. "How is he?" "Do you know his name?" "Where does he come from? Outer space?" "There are rumours saying he was born from a whale, are they true?" "How could he be born from a whale and wear the army uniform?" etc...

Paul got in his car with some difficulty, he started the engine and drove away in his turn.

*

Paul arrived home. He parked his car in front of his house, got out of it quickly, walked to the door, opened it and entered the house. It was a huge, white, hi-tech, one-storey building, based in a residential area of the city, with some panels on its flat roof to feed it with solar energy, and several satellite dishes, some of them able to pick up commercial messages and spread them inside, across the walls. A very private and expensive service.

Even before closing the door: "Laura?" he called.

"Yeah?" his wife's voice sounded.

"Okay." He closed the door.

One of his two house employees came to him. It

was a tan, short woman. Her name was Renee, 49. "She's upstairs, sir," she said to him.

"She'd better be." He looked around. "Did you shut off all the advertising aerials, as I asked you to on the phone?"

"Yes, sir. It's done."

"Perfect," he said, nodding. "Thank you." He ran upstairs. "Where are you?" he exclaimed.

"In the spare bedroom," Laura said.

There were five bedrooms across the house, four on the upper floor (and three of them left unoccupied), the fifth one on the ground level, used by the two employees. Paul entered the spare bedroom, now occupied. "How is he?"

The boy was lying on his back, in a double bed. Laura was just standing in front of the bed, watching him, her face expressionless.

"Still unconscious, what do you think?" she replied provocatively. "Ask him if you can."

"I'm not the one who found him."

"What, you think he was conscious when I found him? You think I knocked him down?"

"Maybe your friend did. By accident. Or on purpose."

"Don't you have any other idea about what happened to him?" she asked, more seriously.

"No," he said, "but I've heard the radio."

"And?"

"Have you heard anything since you got here?" He looked at the boy.

"I was too busy with him."

"Well, something kind of weird just came out,"

he said. "I heard it on the radio a few minutes ago, on the way. The army is talking about a 16-year-old kid from Arkansas, missing for over 20 years, since some cyclone came through and blew away everything around, including some army base."

"And they think it might be him?"

"Yes," he said, nodding. "Also, there is a couple, now claiming to be his parents. You know, father and mother. They are from Arkansas too. The thing is, they are about 60 years old."

"They're 60?"

"Yeah."

"Did the army provide a name?" she asked.

"Yes." He had another look at the boy. "Charlie... Bradshaw. Something like that."

"What about the police?"

"I don't know, they still aren't saying anything, so I believe there's still nothing about him in their files."

"Are you telling me he came over here through time?" Laura asked after a short moment.

"Time *and space,*" he answered. "That's what the army is saying, not me."

"This is a crazy story!" she exclaimed.

"If you say so."

"Bullshit for the tourists," she added.

"Yeah!" he nodded.

"Do you believe it?"

"Of course not."

"Nobody will go for it."

"Everybody might," he said, "when the uniform the boy was wearing is checked, and the name on it confirmed. The uniform was for committed volunteer soldiers, and that missing kid was one of them."

Laura turned round eyes to the coma boy. "How old did you say he'd be?"

"Er… 16," he said.

"That's impossible," she said, shaking her head.

"When you found him, he was wearing the uniform, yes or no?" he asked.

"Yes, but… it just can't be!" She now looked totally confused.

"Look, I have a press conference now." He left the room, Laura followed him after a last glance at the kid.

On the landing he stopped and turned to her. "Aren't you angry with me?" he asked her.

"Sorry?"

"You won't be taking him somewhere else, will you?"

"What are you talking about?" she asked, disconcerted.

"I never know with you. But I know how things go when you're pissed."

"I'm not pissed!"

"Then what's been making you see somebody else?"

"You see?" she said, upset. "Some good time to talk about this again, when we need each other for this kid."

"Some good reason to talk it over again, for the good of the kid."

"It's because things like that, that I left you in the end."

"You didn't leave me," he corrected. "You cheated on me."

"Is there a difference?"

"Sure. You're still here," he said, grinning a little.

"If you keep going this way, I really will take the boy away from here."

Paul walked away, followed by Laura. Then he went down the stairs, still followed by Laura.

"And you know what?" she added. "I think it's what you want me to do, in a way."

"Oh, really?" he said, still going down.

"Yeah. And this is the problem I have with you."

"Wrong point there. I'm just asking myself a valuable question."

They reached the hall. Once there they stopped and turned to each other.

"You always say you don't like kids," she said, "and that you don't want any, and yet you run a foundation for the needy. I imagine, for kids, too."

"And?"

"I'd like to know my husband a little better."

"I've told you already," he told her. "I love kids when they're not under my roof."

"Then why did you bring that one in here?" she asked.

"For a reason you can't get. He doesn't belong to me. And he's precisely a needy one. He won't stay here forever anyway."

"That you don't know about."

"We'll continue arguing about this later, okay? I need to call my press agent."

"Sure."

"Now you're angry with me."

"Get outta here, Paul."

"Can I rely on you?" he asked.

"Sure," she said. "I'm still your wife. But you may have a surprise when you get back."

He came to her and kissed her softly. "You'll never understand me, will you?" he asked her.

"I don't understand you... so far."

"But it doesn't mean you don't feel anything for me."

"A woman is full of surprises."

Paul gently stepped away from her. Then, unexpectedly: "Renee!" he called.

Renee finally showed up. "Yes?"

"Can you do me a favour?" Paul asked her.

"Sure thing, sir."

"Watch this woman close," he told her. "You have my permission. If she ever does anything terrible, feel free to call me. Or the fire department."

"I may knock her down before she does," Laura said to him.

Paul grinned again. "You do that and I sue you for staff damaging," he said. Then he left, closing the door behind him.

The two women looked at each other, kind of stunned.

II

Press conference. Paul was standing in the main room of his own foundation, on a slightly raised platform, in front of a microphone and a crowd of journalists, cameramen and photographers. The whole scene was looking like to happen at the White House, with Paul as the president.

"I guess the kid is still unconscious," he said. "I'm not in the right place to check. According to all the doctors at the hospital, he could wake up at any time. There's nothing wrong with him actually."

A male reporter in the back of the room raised his hand and was allowed to ask: "Why did you take him with you? Without warning anybody in or outside of the hospital?"

"I had no real reason to do that. I mean, to warn anybody." There were some protests that Paul calmed down. "When politicians make decisions they are not asked to warn anybody outside the Senate or the White House before, right? Well, it's the same thing here."

There were more protests. "You're not a politician!" another male reporter said, without being allowed to talk.

"I'm in charge, just like them," he said to this. "I was concerned about the kid. That's all. As you probably know, there were some weird people making a scene in front of the hospital. They wanted the kid, and I guess they still do. Again, I was concerned."

"Which people are you talking about, mister?" the same reporter asked.

"You know that. You guys were there when they called my wife a sinner and almost threatened me. They also told me about the plans they have for the kid. You saw, heard and recorded everything, you took photos. I guess you did."

This time there was some murmuring of embarrassment. Nobody responded.

"Was it the only reason?" another one asked him.

"No. As I said, there's nothing wrong with him. Physically, I mean. So I thought it would be better for him if he woke up in a normal house instead of in a hospital, that's why I decided to take him with me and bring him to my home."

"You made the decision all by yourself?" another journalist asked.

"Yes, but I had to be given the permissions. My wife was also present."

"You didn't care about others' opinions, I mean, non-medical ones?" another one asked.

"Nobody non-medical came for the kid. Nobody really cares."

This time there was some laughing mixed with protests.

"This makes the kid more than public. He belongs to the masses," the same reporter said. "To everybody!"

"No, I don't agree," Paul said, shaking his head vigorously. "I don't agree at all. The fact is, nobody cares, but everybody wants to see him, everybody wants a piece of him, everybody wants a show out of this, right? And that's too many opinions to handle anyway. Only the future will tell us if I did right or wrong."

"What do you mean, mister?"

"As long as he's in a coma, yes, I guess he belongs to all of us. This will change when he wakes up, if he ever does. Then he'll be his own person, more private than anything else. That's what I thought about. I only showed some care and respect for a person, for a human being we don't know anything about yet. A young stranger, a puppet for most. So I'm asking you this: are you guys going to show the same?"

*

"You just heard a part of a press conference hosted by Mister Paul Ingrams himself and held inside his foundation, a few hours ago, in the heart of San Francisco. He assumed total responsibility for his actions. For him, the kid needs to be taken care of within a normal, well-off family, not to be some American Idol, and be used and followed as such an idol by the media when he can't say and do anything about it. Barbara Bergman, San Francisco, CNN."

That was two hours later. With Paul being at home, seated beside Laura on a couch, in front of a large, flat screen TV set, wall-embedded, showing the news. The voice they were hearing was from a woman, a journalist.

A couple of reporters hosting the news show, took over. They were smiling with great humour, like the case wasn't as serious as it seemed.

"Thank you very much, Barbara," the man said. "Now the question is, and the question Mister Ingrams could ask himself, is: did he draw more media, press and popular attention to the kid by taking him away from the hospital to his own home?"

"In my opinion he certainly did," the woman followed, "by trying to take the kid away from the media spotlight, he did the opposite, he made the kid even more famous and wanted. That kid is a total, complete mystery, and we, the public, the audience, we all love it! We all want to know what his story is! He can't keep it all for himself!"

"Can you change this, please?" Paul asked Laura.

"You have the control," she said with some amusement.

"Oh yeah," he said. The press conference had gone on and put him in bad enough mood, so he almost had a car accident on his way back home.

He used the remote control to switch off the TV, and Laura chuckled. "I can't believe this…" he said.

"Don't you find this kind of normal?"

"What?" he exclaimed, looking at her.

The home phone rang, it stopped after a few seconds.

"They just need to see if the boy is all right," she said.

Paul disagreed immediately. "No, it means they can't trust a guy like me, a respected businessman who runs a well-known foundation, to care about him and make sure everything is okay. That, or they just wanna peep and have fun."

"You're too hard on people."

"D'you remember what happened after Michael Jackson died? All his kids under real TV show cameras, when they were still under age? They all just want the same thing here. And you think it's normal? You think it's right?" he said heavily. So heavily that Laura didn't say anything to this. "It's a goddamned shame, yes."

"What can you do about it anyway?" she said. "You're not the boy's father. You have no authority over him."

"You think those guys have more authority than me?"

"It's up to the kid, Paul. Not you."

"Right now it's more up to them. I just wanna protect him from people like them."

"Again, you're not his father, you can't make all

87

the decisions for him. You can't be the only person on this earth allowed to see him."

He looked at her for a short moment. "Yeah..." he sighed. "I guess you have a point here."

"Let go, Paul. Don't be paranoid."

"You know what? You just made me think of something... since I came back here I haven't seen the boy even once..." He stood up right away and ran to the stairs. Catching Laura totally off guard.

"Hey!" she exclaimed. She stood up in her turn and ran after him. He started running up the stairs and she followed, running as well. "Paul, please stop it!"

Once on the first floor he entered the boy's bedroom. Renee and the other house employee were there. A man, called Travis, 52. Also tan and short, and from Puerto Rico, just like her.

The boy was still lying unconscious on the bed, covered with a heavy duvet. Paul looked at him. "Know what?" he said again. "I've never thought before about how cute that boy really is."

"Will you cut that shit out?" Laura said, desperately.

"You think I'm fooling around? Well, maybe I am, after all."

"You're really sounding like a kid, you know that?"

"He *is* cute, mister," Renee said. "He reminds me of my son, when he was about his age."

Laura shook her head with some exasperation.

"How old is your son now?" Paul asked Renee.

"He's 28."

"We still don't know how old this kid is."

"Oh, he can't be over 17," Renee said with much certitude.

"We've received many phone calls tonight, sir," Travis said to Paul.

"I know. Did you take any of them?"

"I took all of them, from up here."

"And…?"

Travis shrugged. "Every call was for you," he said. "But I never called for you because there was nothing interesting."

"Good," Paul said, nodding. "Very good." He walked out of the room, followed by Laura. Once on the landing he stopped and turned to her. "You told me not to be paranoid," he told her, "I'm not. You're the one who's being naive here. You really think that nothing will happen to the kid? You think there are only angels out there?" The home phone rang. "Shit." He walked to their bedroom. Laura followed.

"I know that, Paul," she said. "Most of them wish to make money out of him. I'm not that naive."

Paul reached to a bedside table with a ringing phone on it. He turned the loud speaker on, then he picked up the receiver, keeping it away from his ear.

There was a loud voice coming out of the speaker: "Watch for the day He'll wake up! Then we'll all be judged!"

Paul hung up. "Did you hear that?" he asked.

"I did. I'm not deaf either, Paul." She was kind of smiling.

"Do you find this funny?"

"Don't you?"

"No. Of course not! Not at all."

"You're taking things much too seriously."

"We're talking about the safety of a kid, that's a serious matter. These are the kind of crazies I'm worried about the most."

"So?" Laura said, shrugging.

"So?" he said as an echo. "How did they get this land line number? It's not listed."

"Maybe somebody in your staff is a crazy himself," she said.

"And I shouldn't take that seriously? Shit," he said again.

"Too bad you don't want any videophone in here."

He sighed. "Okay, you're not deaf and not that naive. And I may be too serious, too careful, to be totally rational. So you tell me, what are we supposed to do?"

*

The next morning, Paul and Laura had moved the boy to another furnished house, smaller than theirs but still big, somewhere in the suburbs of San Francisco. They had made a decision.

The place was now crowded with TV workers from Fox News, who were turning it into some kind of a studio. They were busy putting cameras everywhere, hiding them carefully inside boxes and closets, or behind all kinds of objects.

Laura was busy supervising the setting, walking around the place, watching the whole thing. She didn't have much to say or argue about; as a matter of fact, she said almost nothing. She was not a specialist.

A little before noon, Paul, who had rented the house in a hurry the night before, and a Fox executive were sitting around a table, in the living room.

"So we agree on this, right?" Paul asked.

"Yeah, yeah," the executive said.

"If anything ever happens in here," Paul warned, "if strangers break in this place and turn it upside down, it will mean that something went wrong with your team, that somebody inside opened his or her mouth too wide, you'll be responsible and I'll take you and all your fellow executives or whatever to court, you hear?"

"You don't have to repeat it a thousand times," the executive groaned, "I got it, dammit!"

"Just making sure."

"What if the kid wakes up now?" the exec suggested.

"Just pray he doesn't as long as you guys are in here, and hope he doesn't stay in a coma too long, or the viewers may find your show more boring than hell, you'll get lousy ratings and lose lots of money, that's all you can do now!" Paul didn't have any more time to waste with that guy. He stood up and walked away.

The Fox team kept operating.

The boy, still unconscious, was lying on a different bed, covered with different sheets and blankets. His bedroom had already been set up.

There were three video cameras hidden in his bedroom. All pointed at the bed with the kid lying on it, showing him from very different angles but from distances that were nearly the same.

Paul and Laura were having a conversation in private. The Fox staff was still in the house so they had to whisper, also to look around them as well, making sure nobody was filming or listening.

"I hope you knew what you were doing," Laura said.

"What do you mean?"

"Renting this different location…"

"We've already talked it over."

"That won't keep people from coming to our place."

"That will keep them away from the kid," Paul said. "You know that."

"A press conference won't be enough. Anyway."

"Who told you about a press conference? I certainly won't call one about this place."

"Whatever."

"We'll see what happens. Let go. Just like you said. You agreed to this shit, remember?" Paul reminded her.

Laura sighed. She was not tired.

"What's the matter with you?" Paul asked.

"What about your friend, Stuart? What does he think of this?"

"I haven't talked with him for a while," Laura said.

"I suppose he's been calling you and…"

"He's not been calling," she corrected.

"Have *you* been calling?" he asked. As Laura shrugged a no: "You forget your friends fast. I recall you forgot about me for a while too."

"Would you like to see him here?" she asked.

"I won't invite him. I don't give a shit if you do. Anyway I don't understand what's happening to you. You should be happy, you're gonna be able to kind of act and be some star."

"If you really believe that's what I'm interested in, you're deadly wrong."

"Don't be a hypocrite. Look, I gotta go now."

"Okay."

"Good luck."

"Thanks."

"See you on TV."

"Right."

Paul left the place, followed by Laura's eyes.

Then Laura entered the boy's bedroom and had a seat on a chair. From where she was seated she could see TV people working outside the room, moving around the place. She wasn't paying much attention to them any more.

Her eyes drifted to the unconscious kid lying on the bed. She knew there was a video camera just above her, catching him in the frame and watching him almost the same way she was watching him.

*

Two days later, the place was totally deserted, except for Laura and the kid. And nothing had happened. Absolutely nothing. Which was normal since nobody knew where the show was taking place, except Paul and Laura. But the video cameras from Fox News were still there, watching and waiting. Especially the ones in the kid's bedroom. Laura was sleeping in her bedroom. With two cameras pointed straight at her uncovered body.

So nothing had happened for two days, but the ratings were still quite high and Fox was very happy. The executives had created a series of derivative, paying channels operating through the satellite network, exclusively for what had been called "The Beach Boy Real Show". Those channels were broadcasting the show permanently, with short, regular reports on Fox during every commercial break. Despite the total lack of action, the show was working great because the viewers were only waiting for the boy to wake up, move in his bed and start 'talking'. That was the only thing that seemed to matter for them about the show, and strangely (and Paul was wrong on this point), the longer the show was lasting, the more they were showing patience and feeling passion and tension. Nobody, or almost nobody, was getting bored, the view of the boy lying totally motionless in his bed – after two days he hadn't moved an inch – and Laura walking around in the place and living like anybody else did, was largely enough. Because Laura was another character that was worth watching, especially when she was entering the bathroom – the Fox guys of course didn't tell her, but they'd hidden a micro-camera in that room.

It was late in the morning when she opened her eyes, woke up and got off the bed – then walked out of the room.

She checked the boy's bedroom. She walked to the bed, watching the kid. This lasted one long minute, then she left.

She went downstairs, entered the kitchen, opened the fridge and took a couple of eggs out of it. The cameras set high up in the room caught her breaking them in a saucepan.

The minute after she was in the living room, an egg sandwich in one hand, using her other hand and a remote control to switch on the TV set and change channels, looking for something interesting. After a little while she found what could be called 'Beach Boy TV', showing her live on the show, standing in the living, then Charlie lying on his bed, still in his coma, not moving.

Some of the other channels were broadcasting sitcoms, commercials, games, soap operas... and sort of a debate between two men of science.

"...saying that the theory that is commonly

accepted today is impossible from my point of view."

"What theory? We're talking about what we know. About what the army told us. This is all we have so far."

"This is total science-fiction! Space-time! What the army said can't validate what we're talking about. Think about this, with all the technology we have we couldn't find a way to travel through time yet. And you're asking me to believe that a teenager from the deep Midwest has been able to make a big jump through time *and* space, just like that? This is too big to be true."

Laura stayed on that one.

"So? Are you telling us that the army is nothing but a bunch of storytelling mythomaniacs? Is that what you're saying?"

"Did you read or see *The Time Machine*?"

"Of course, like everybody else."

"Or like anybody who knows H.G. Wells, that's not everybody."

"Everybody knows about that book and about the classic story it tells!"

"Anyway, his book shows time travel that doesn't include space. The guy makes big jumps through time but basically he doesn't move, him and the machine stay at the exact same place during the travel."

"It's only a fiction story! You said it yourself, we've never been able to find a way to travel through time, and you're trying to make us believe that a fiction book has all the right answers…!"

"Time travel just can't include space, that's the only point I'm trying to bring here."

"What do you know about that? You can't be certain of it, you've never witnessed such a thing, nobody else has. Okay, I'm gonna do just like you and use fiction to bring some strength to my arguments, did you read or see *Time after Time*?"

"No, what is it?"

"It's another science-fiction book, much less known, from a novelist named Karl Alexander, published in 1979, taken to the screen the following year, and showing H.G. Wells himself as the hero who actually did build a time machine, and Jack the Ripper using it to escape from the police. And guess what? He travels through time and space! Jumping from 1893's London to 1979's San Francisco. How's that? What do you have to say about this?"

"You mean that the time machine built by Wells in that story… is actually a *space-time* machine?"

"Precisely!"

"It doesn't make any sense to me. It was purely impossible to build such a machine at that time."

"Once again, the story is purely fictive. What about what happened to the kid?"

"Some more recent movies like *Back to the Future* or *The Terminator* don't show time travel that includes space."

"This is true, but let's forget about fiction. What about the kid?"

"I guess we need to wait until he wakes up, that's all we can do."

"What about the uniform he was wearing? He was missing for twenty years, in Arkansas…"

"I know that. And we definitely know that he didn't use any machine to make his so-called jump. If he had, we would have seen it. Unless that girl with glasses was right about that big fall from the sky, which means the machine will have to be found at the very deep bottom of the Pacific."

"What do you think happened to him inside that tornado?"

"Or what might have happened to him inside that tornado. I don't know of course but I have a theory about this, a purely scientific theory. Any matter disintegrates and creates its anti-matter, that's the base of nuclear physics. It's very possible for us now to disintegrate a particle or any living thing at one point, and to reintegrate it totally at another point, without dealing with its total anti-particle."

"You're talking about basic teleportation."

"It's not that basic. What I want to say is, it's still impossible to do that and at the same time, to make that particle or living thing jump through time."

"We don't know everything yet, and I guess we'll never know everything, especially about this. If we did, all researchers and scientists could retire for ever or look for another job. Nature is what it is. We'll never get all the answers."

"And the kid, what if he was sort of a… a nature's reject? Again, apparently he achieved something that we're still totally unable to do, with all the technology we have. What he would have to say to us could be the proof that fiction has joined reality and made it even more fantastic…"

Laura changed the channel and, after a short moment, she switched off the TV and left the living room. She went back upstairs, then back into Charlie's bedroom, walking to the bed, staring at his totally still body.

"When are you gonna wake up, kiddo?" she said.

Same day, early in the afternoon.

Laura was standing in the living room. On the phone. Her cell phone. The home phone could be bugged, she didn't know how to check it so she wasn't using it. Not for the moment, as long as there were cameras in the house, with her inside.

"Don't call again. I mean it," she was saying. "Yes, I do mean it," she continued after a beat. "I will call you. I promise. I just can't do it now. You know the reason."

"Yes, I know. I'm not stupid," Stuart said. "Look, I'm outside your house."

There were many people and a lot of noise around him. Laura could hear the noisy background.

"Yeah?" she said.

"Yeah. I suppose you know, there's some kind of a demonstration in front. And all around too, probably."

"Thanks for the info," she said. "I have a husband, he already let me know."

"What d'you mean by that, he let you know?" he

asked, frowning. There was no response for a moment. "Hello?"

"Yes," she said timidly. She had realized the mistake she had just made. But it was too late to undo it.

"You're not in the house with him," he quickly concluded. "And the kid either. The show doesn't take place here, right?" There was another moment with no response from Laura. So he continued. "Of course it doesn't. We've all been fooled. But I understand. The kid's safety first."

"What are you gonna do?" she asked. After a short pause: "You know I can't."

"Tell me where you are, Laura. I need to see you."

"I don't care. I just can't. You know why. Don't be such a pain."

"Look, the demonstration… it's a supportive one," he announced. "Like a protest."

"I know that too," she said.

"I can guess they all run for Paul, they don't approve what's going on. What about you, Laura? Do you approve it?"

"What I may think doesn't matter," she said.

"It does to me. Your husband was against this from the very beginning."

"I know. How many of you are out there?" she asked.

"Not enough to stop the show."

"Did they spot you? Do they know who you are?"

"I changed my face and put sunglasses on. I told

you, I'm not stupid. So you don't wanna tell me where you are?" he asked again.

Laura got irritated by this insistent question. "For the last time, I can't. Can't you understand that?"

"And I can't have your opinion either, about what's going on and you being on camera?"

Laura hung up. "Fuckin' stupid," she said. She knew she was on camera but at the moment she was upset enough not to care. It didn't matter anyway. After all, everybody already knew she was married and had a relationship with somebody else. The story had been in every newspaper all across the country.

She started walking again, pocketing the phone and heading to the door, when there was a new ring. Her cell phone. Again. She knew who it was.

She took it out and after a motionless moment, decided to take the call.

"You still don't get it, do you…" she said.

"Laura, you're not leaving me any choice."

"What do you mean?"

"Tell me where you and the kid are or I'll tell everybody out here that both of you are in some other place."

Laura almost exploded. "You do that shit and you'll never see me again. Ever!"

"Look, we found the kid together, I have the right to know where he is, and where you are."

"Yes, you do, but not now!!" she cried.

"Listen, Laura…"

"I'll call you later, at the right moment, okay? I promise. Now leave me alone."

"We found him together!" Stuart sounded with passion.

"Oh, you wanna be part of the show too, right? You think I'm enjoying this situation? In case you forgot, I'm not married to you. And the whole world is watching me!"

"Please…"

"You wanna get famous? Go to the police, or to some casting call, and start yelling out, I don't give a shit!" She hung up again, now really pissed. And left the living room.

She started climbing the stairs, and entered the room. The boy was still unconscious. Completely still. She watched him for a short moment, then she walked to a small TV set and turned it on.

*

An hour later she was still in the bedroom, still watching TV, using a small remote control to change channels. She could see herself on Beach Boy TV, like in a mirror. Sitting on the edge of the bed with the boy lying on it, in the background or on the other side of the screen.

Soon there was a sudden program interruption and a news break flashed up on one of the channels. A rather old man was hosting it.

"We have some fresh, and I suppose astounding news about the mystery beach boy," the anchorman announced. "The army just positively identified him as Charlie Bradshaw, a young committed soldier from Arkansas, missing for a little over 20 years, after the army barracks he was in were destroyed by a tornado back then. He was the only person missing from the disaster. The boy was first identified through his fingerprints, but his family still had to uncover many photographs, videos and military clothes, among other things, for the ID to be definitive."

Laura opened her mouth and eyes wide, unable to believe this.

The boy they were talking about was lying behind her, she didn't see him pop his eyes open.

What she was seeing were images rolling on her screen, as the anchorman kept speaking. Images that were not totally new for her since she'd already seen them before, but it was a very long time ago, when she was only a teenager. Seeing them again now was a shock. Images of destruction, of what was left of a military base in the Midwest. She could see firemen working in the rubble, walking across them or using cranes, all of them trying to move the rubble away, less in order to clear the scene than to try to find the only person missing from the disaster, another teenager called Charlie Bradshaw. Some witnesses had seen him being taken away by the tornado but there had still been some hope to finally find him, or at least his body. She knew the search had been fruitless.

Unofficially, Charlie Bradshaw was missing.

Officially, he was dead.

"Now the question is," the anchorman continued, "how the boy could have ended up in San Francisco 21 years later, alive, apparently in perfect condition, and without aging, it's a complete mystery. He's been recovering, still in a coma, at the property of Paul Ingrams, a philanthropic businessman who seems to care a lot about him and his safety. A popular decision resulted in the boy remaining under the eyes of many TV cameras that have been set all across the Ingrams' home…"

Laura could feel some movement from behind, she turned round.

Charlie had half-stood up in his bed. His eyes were wide open, staring into emptiness.

Laura got caught totally off guard by this. She couldn't believe this vision any better. That he was awake now. "Oh…" was all she was able to say at this moment.

She put down the TV volume, stood up and rushed to him, but she didn't touch him.

The boy was looking like he was in some kind of trance. He kept looking at something without seeing it, not seeing Laura. She didn't know what to do. So she didn't do anything.

Until he started blinking. And breathing, too. He turned his head and saw Laura. She smiled at him. "Hey…" she said gently.

She still didn't dare touch him. She only waited for him to say something. Finally: "Hey," he said.

"How are you doing?"

Charlie looked around him, then at the bed he was still on, then around him again, without responding immediately. Then back at Laura. "Where are we?" he asked, very naturally.

"San Francisco, in a house," she said. "Boy, how are you doing? I need to know."

"I'm okay I guess," Charlie replied. "Need to make sure."

"Try to get off the bed," she suggested.

"Okay." He got off the bed rather easily. He tested himself standing, then walking some around the room, along the bed. He felt all right.

"Is it finished?" he suddenly asked, innocently.

"Sorry?"

"The earthquake. Is it finished?" he asked again.

"What earthquake?" she asked in her turn, frowning.

"I saw it happening...," he said after a moment, "here, here in this city."

"What are you talking about?"

"The whole city... down." He looked up at her. "You mean it didn't happen?"

"Nothing that serious happened!" she said with a definitive tone.

"Then it will," he said, as definitively. He lowered his head, frowning. "In one day or two. Tomorrow, I should say."

"You sure you're all right, kid?" she asked, suddenly worried.

"I'm fine," he said. "I'm not joking."

"All right, boy. What's your name?"

"What's yours?" he retorted.

"Sorry," she said. "My name is Laura. Laura Ingrams."

Charlie seemed to be thinking about what to say in return. "My name… well…" he hesitated… suddenly he held his head with his both hands. Laura caught him before he could collapse. "Hey, hey!" She laid him on the bed. But Charlie recovered quickly and got back on his feet.

"You're not fine, kid," she said.

"I am," he assured her, "it's all right."

"I mean, look at you…"

"No, you listen to this, 'cause you need to know. There's gonna be a big earthquake here in a couple of days…"

"Oh really?"

"Yes! I would say tomorrow. More probably in the morning. I saw it happening as soon as I woke up… and I just had another flash of it."

"A flash? Where?"

"Well… in my head," he answered, shrugging.

"In your head…?"

"Well… yes."

"Just your imagination, kid," she said, trying to sound peaceful.

"I'd like it to be just imagined, but no," he said. "It's gonna get real."

"Okay, now look. You just woke up and the first thing you were able to tell me is terrible news that didn't happen and probably won't happen before a long time."

"It will happen!" he exclaimed. "Very soon!"

"All right. Now, tell me something else. Your name, for instance. Do you have a name?"

Almost immediately, a phone rang. It was the

home phone. Laura didn't move at once, still staring at Charlie. Because he still didn't answer her question. He was looking uncomfortable about something. The home phone kept ringing, insistently, so she finally walked away from him, leaving the room.

She entered her bedroom and took the call. "Hello?"

"Mrs. Ingrams?" a voice said.

"Yes, who is this?"

"Fox. The show is over."

"What?"

"It's over."

"Why?"

"You know why. Or did you already forget what the boy just said?" the voice asked.

"He only imagined," she said, "it's okay…"

"He just emerged from a coma, he has no reason to imagine and make jokes. We can't afford to continue and start a general panic. It's over. Our last word."

"Look, mister…"

But the Fox guy, whoever he was, didn't let her continue. "We gave you a plan…" his voice sounded.

"Yes…" she approved.

"Use it to get the cameras, then unplug them, put them into bags and leave the bags outside, in front of your door. You have fifteen minutes." There was another ring. "We're on our way to get them back," the Fox voice finished. "Don't let the boy see us." The guy hung up.

107

The other ring came from Laura's pocket. From her cell phone. She took it out. And took the call.

"Hello Paul…" she said.

"Laura…" He was inside his office, working. And watching what was going on with his wife and the mystery boy, on television. He'd seen what happened when the boy had woken up and started talking.

"I suppose you heard it…" she said.

"You suppose right, I heard it," he said. He was sounding weird. "Everybody heard it! Everybody across the country, maybe even beyond!"

"Hey, don't start to panic!"

"I'm not panicking," he retorted.

"You're sounding so. Listen, they just stopped the show."

"Really?"

"Yeah… they just called me."

"I see."

"Did they call you?" she asked.

"Absolutely not."

There was a moment of tense silence.

"Paul?"

"I'm here. Now look Laura…"

"I'm listening."

"When they cancel a show without any notice," he said, "it's usually in order to replace it with another one."

"What are you…"

"I know those guys. I know how they think and reason. Everything for profit. Especially fear, whoever feels it, themselves included."

"They told me to get the cameras back and to put them outside…"

"Don't do that," he said immediately. "Just take the boy and get out of the house with him, before they show up. Don't wait." He hung up.

Laura stood completely still for a short moment, seeming to be intensively thinking. About two completely different things she was just told to do.

Charlie's voice woke her up. "Laura?"

Laura turned round. Charlie was standing in the doorway, looking at her. "Who was supposed to hear what?" he asked.

She walked to him. "Nothing…" she said.

"What about a show? Cameras?"

"Forget it for the moment. Go back to your room, open the closet, pick up some clothes and go to the bathroom and get dressed. And please do it quickly. We're leaving."

"Where?"

"As I said. Now."

Charlie left the room.

He entered his bedroom, went to the closet, opened it and chose among the clothes inside.

As he did, Laura grabbed the two cameras in her room, she turned them off, unplugged them and left the room with them.

On the landing she could reach another camera, set high up. One of the TV crew members gave her a plan just before they left the place, so she already knew where to find all the cameras. Almost all.

She had an eye on Charlie's bedroom. The kid was still busy inside. "Hurry, kid," she said.

Soon Charlie left the room with some clothes in his arms. Laura showed him a door. "The bathroom is here…" she told him.

He walked to the door, and entered the bathroom, closing the door behind him.

Then Laura walked into his bedroom. And she looked at the TV screen. She checked the Beach Boy channels and saw a series of black screens. Then she went back on Fox. The news break was over but there hadn't been any report, the show was not back on the air – it had really been stopped. She looked away as some family sitcom was starting, with its opening credits rolling.

She grabbed the three cameras and unplugged them, then she quickly left the room.

A moment later she was going downstairs, carrying two big, full bags. Once in the hall she put them down on the floor, then she switched on the light, opened the entrance door and looked outside.

Nobody yet.

She put the two bags outside, without stepping out. Then she closed the door.

"Boy?" she called.

"Yes…?" his voice sounded from upstairs.

"Are you ready?"

"Almost!"

"Hurry, let's go!" She entered the living room and switched two lamps on.

As she got back into the hall... Charlie came down.

"Good," she said, grabbing his arm. "This way." She took him to the back of the house.

"Why?" he asked.

She didn't say anything, she only picked up her own handbag and left the house with him through the back door, locking the door, leaving some lights on in the house and the TV set on in the spare bedroom.

"This way," she said, pointing toward some point.

They had to get across the property, which was protected along its back side. Not in the front.

"Don't you have a car?" Charlie asked.

"We'll walk, Charlie."

"Charlie?"

She looked at him. "Yeah..." she said with a sigh. "That's your name."

"I don't remember it..."

"You don't?"

Charlie shook his head.

"Whatever. Let's get outta here," she said.

A small wooden door opened in a wall, and Charlie and Laura got out, ending up on the sidewalk. The area was half-residential. She used a key to lock the door behind them.

Then they started walking down the street.

She heard a noise, so she walked around the corner and back to their main street. Then she stopped as she noticed some people in front of the house, and saw some other people riding along the street and stopping in front of the same house. Most of them were TV workers. Her face tensed up with anger. She knew what it meant. Exactly what Paul had said. Now that the show was over, the Fox executives had opened their mouths and spread the word about the real location.

"What's happening?" Charlie asked, not understanding anything.

"Let's go," Laura just said.

They walked away without being noticed.

"Laura, can you tell me where we're going?"

"We're going away from those people."

"To where?"

Laura smiled slightly. "Somewhere downtown."

"Are we walking all the way?"

"Sorry about that, but yes."

"How far is it?"

She stopped smiling. "Far enough for us to get the time we need to talk." After a moment walking: "You know what's odd?" she asked suddenly. Charlie shook his head again. "You emerged from your coma just as your identity was coming up on TV…" she said slowly.

This was just an observation, and she didn't say anything more, not expecting Charlie to explain himself, knowing very well he wouldn't be able to say anything specific about this.

"Really?" was all he could say.

It was probably just a coincidence.

III

Laura and Charlie had found seats inside the Museum of Modern Art, based in downtown San Francisco. Laura was holding an evening edition of a newspaper which had just come out. Both of them were wearing sunglasses. In order not to be recognized. There was nobody else sitting on the same bench. As Laura was reading the paper, Charlie was looking around, fascinated.

And puzzled. Since he woke up and had the prediction, he was totally unable to remember anything from his past. Nothing and nobody was coming, his mind was a blank. All along the way to the museum they hadn't had the conversation Laura had meant to have. She had been too busy making sure the way was clear to say anything. And Charlie had been too busy keeping his head up, his mouth and eyes wide open, discovering the new world he had just entered, to say anything more. A short time before they had reached downtown, Laura had given Charlie one of her pair of sunglasses and put another pair on, then she had bought the newspaper, and they had read the article about him together, inside the museum, sitting on the bench. He was making the headlines. Once they had finished, Laura had said that the whole article was based on information that was not confirmed. Then she'd told him about everything (true events) that had happened from the moment she found him on the shore; finally she asked Charlie about his thoughts and he hadn't said anything. But he did have some thoughts.

So he was, or used to be, a US Army soldier from Arkansas – only at age 16. And he'd been taken away by a cyclone. According to some witnesses, who were soldiers like him, he had thrown himself into it more than anything else. Then nothing, no news at all, during twenty-one long years, until a former athlete got her feet mixed up over his soaked body, on a California beach. There was some bimbo with sunglasses who was still saying, over and over again, that he might have fallen down straight into the water from the sky. His unknown, unidentified status, along with his young age, had been exploited by a mainstream TV channel which had organized a national show and pointed its cameras at him when he was in bed, still in a coma.

The more he thought about this story, the more he found it funny.

Until he remembered that this funny story was his. And he felt nothing, except a great emptiness. He was a total stranger, a young outcast in a strange place, more alone than anybody else could be. How could he have ended up here anyway, when according to the first news in the paper, he was living thousands of miles away? And what happened to him during those twenty-one years? He was totally unable to remember anything about this either.

As he was feeling so sorry for himself, unsuccessfully trying to remember something, Laura was reading the article once more.

They were sitting on that bench for a while, over an hour. Laura suddenly closed the paper and turned to Charlie. He still wasn't saying anything. Laura didn't want to force him. But after a moment she couldn't stop herself.

"So? Don't you have anything to say?" she asked.

"I don't know what to say," he said. "And even if I did know…"

"Well…"

"You're telling me there were TV cameras in my bedroom…"

"There were TV cameras all over the house," she specified, "but your bedroom was the main subject here."

"What am I supposed to say about it?" he asked. "Or to do?"

"I don't know, it's up to you, Charlie."

"What difference would it make?"

"None. I know. Apparently they don't care. There's not much movement outside."

"They don't believe me."

"I guess they don't."

"You don't either."

"I don't know what to believe."

"This place is safe," Charlie said.

"Yeah…?"

"I mean, until the earthquake destroys it."

"So what do you suggest? That we stay here until it happens? We can't."

"I don't have anything to suggest. If I did, you wouldn't listen anyway."

"What about the house?" she asked. "Is it safe too?"

"You mean the house we left?"

"Yes."

"Yes, I saw both of us leave it."

She grinned a little. "And that's it."

"Yes, that's it."

"Nothing after that?"

"Nothing."

"I mean, nothing bad?"

"Nothing bad for us," he said.

Laura nodded. "Tell me more about you, Charlie," she said. "If you can."

"I don't have anything to tell you about me. I don't know my name, how old I am, where I come from…"

"I know all that, I just told you everything. I heard it on TV first."

"TV? You mean television? That's nothing to me," he said, shaking his head. "I mean… I'm lost."

"I can help you…"

"No, you can't."

"You still know what will happen to you in the future…"

"No, even that I don't. I mean… I get into some place and I'm able to see whatever will happen in it. That's all I can do, basically."

"I see," she said.

He looked at her. "No, you don't see anything."

"I mean, I understand."

"You understand I'm a loony."

"No Charlie, I don't. You wouldn't be here with me if I did."

"Do you remember everything that happened in your life?" he asked her.

"Of course not."

"Well, I forgot everything. I don't remember anything. What difference does it make?"

"You have a family, Charlie. Parents, a brother, a sister… don't you even remember them?"

"I don't," he answered, shaking his head again.

"Do you know everything that's gonna happen next?"

"You see, you're not listening. I just told you, it depends on the place I'm standing in."

"And when you're standing on the outside?"

"I don't see anything."

"Okay." She held up the paper. "From what's written in this," she said, "your family has grown 21 years older, when you have remained the same. I guess you're still 16. What do you think of it?"

"Nothing, since I don't remember my family."

"Don't you remember anything about the tornado either?"

"You're still not listening."

"Please. Make an effort."

"Are you deaf, or what? I don't remember anything that happened to me since I emerged from the coma. I just don't."

"All right," she said. "Take it easy." She checked her watch and stood up. "I guess this place is about to close. So is my bank. I'm gonna need some cash."

"For what? Renting a space inside here?" he asked, a bit ironically.

Laura looked at him with some surprise, and again showed a little grin. "Yeah." She picked up her bag. "We're outta here. Both of us."

"Where are we going?" Charlie asked, standing up in his turn.

"To the bank. To get some cash." She looked at him again. "Calm down," she said.

"What do you need cash for?"

"We need to find a hotel room and I can't use my name. Usually I use my credit card but right now I can't afford to do that."

"They'll ask for your ID."

"I have a fake one," she specified. "It's useful when you're married to someone with money. It keeps the attention away."

"Who's your husband?" Charlie asked.

"Later."

They left the place without being recognized.

*

After a short time and way walking through very normally crowded streets, with people not looking to be rushing out of town at all, they entered a bank. That time had still been long enough for Charlie to ask himself some questions, after all the ones Laura had asked him without him having been able to answer any of them. He'd ended up wondering what kind of person he had been back then, in Arkansas. He was perfectly aware that he'd been born somewhere. So if it was in that place called Arkansas, why not. From what he'd heard and read so far he could guess he hadn't been so good. Apparently everybody around him had run away from that cyclone, him excepted. He'd also wondered about what to do about his lost memory, if he had to totally forget about his past, to kiss it goodbye, or on the contrary, to try to retrieve and reconstruct it, to stick to what was being said and investigate. This hadn't lasted long. He knew he couldn't decide right away. He still knew too little, notably about himself and his personality and temper – he could guess he lost all that he knew about that too. The future was the key.

That conclusion helped him to relax a little bit and to look ahead. That was all he could do anyway. Look ahead and see what happens.

It was rather crowded inside the bank, too. The desks were all open and busy, and the line-ups were all requiring a 5 to 10-minute wait.

"Dammit!" Laura mumbled. Patience had never been her strong point. Especially when it was about waiting for her turn in a public place.

Charlie suddenly started to collapse, but without losing any of his consciousness. He closed his eyes and held his head with his hands. Despite her frustration, Laura noticed.

"Charlie?" she said. "What's wrong?"

"Laura, we need to get out of here," he said, gasping a little.

"Out of here? Why?" She grabbed him and looked around. "What's the matter with you?" she said in his ear.

"Let's just get out. Please."

"Why?"

"There's going to be a robbery," he said. "Some guys with guns will be in here soon."

She frowned with disbelief. "Are you sure?" she asked.

"Yes, I'm sure."

"How much time?"

"Short time," he replied. "Very short."

"That's enough, Charlie," she said.

"You don't believe me?" he said, looking up incredulously at her.

"Of course I don't. Why should I?"

"Why would I bullshit you?"

"I know you're no psychic."

"You don't know anything about me!"

"I said enough. People are looking at us."

"Okay, you stay in here with them." He turned loose and left the bank.

Leaving her motionless, dumbfounded. "Charlie!" she exclaimed but of course he didn't hear it. Then she looked around her. Some people had turned to her, watching, kind of worried. She regained control and joined the line-up.

Then she had a look at the outside, through the window, looking for Charlie. She didn't see him. "Dammit!" she said again, but for a totally different reason.

After a little while it was her turn. There was a young girl behind the desk. Looked like a teenager.

"Hello…" Laura said.

"Hello."

"I'd like to withdraw… let's say, two hundred dollars."

"Couldn't you get them from the ATM outside?" the teller asked.

"One is out of order, another one doesn't deliver 20-dollar bills. And I want only 20s."

"And the third one?"

"Too many people waiting in front," Laura said.

"Of course." The girl gave Laura a small form. "Fill this out, please. And I'll need your ID."

Soon the girl counted the cash in front of Laura, laying it on the counter. In 20-dollar bills.

"Two hundred," she announced.

"Thank you…" Laura was about to pick it up when…

…there was a big crash, from the entrance door.

"All right, this is a robbery!" a big, strong voice suddenly yelled. "Everybody freeze!"

Laura turned, flabbergasted, her mouth and eyes wide open.

Four hooded people with shotguns had just

broken in. Pointing their guns at everybody in sight. Looking for guys in security uniforms. There were two of them.

The same voice shrieked: "Get down on the floor, now! All of you!"

One of the three other guys spotted a security guard looking for his gun. He fired once, in the air.

Everybody in front of the desks got down on the floor, most of them yelling out – Laura included, without having the time and opportunity to pocket her cash. Everybody except the robbers and the two security guards in the room, at this moment.

The second robber cocked his shotgun and pointed it at the guard, who had just frozen, about to take out his own weapon. "Don't do that," the second robber said harshly, "put your hands in the air!" The guard didn't move an inch. "I said, in the air! Both of them!"

The guard finally obeyed. He put his two hands in the air. Without his gun.

"Put them on your head! Now!" the robber said, and the guard obeyed right away. "Now get down on the floor!" This time the guard kind of took his time. "Are you deaf or d'you wanna get your ass blown away? Down! Now!"

The guard got down on the floor, on his stomach.

"Don't you fuckin' move!" the gangster said.

The third robber was on the other security guard, whose hands were already in the air. He was looking harmless.

"You too! Get your dirty ass down!" the robber said to him.

The other security guard got down on the floor, on his stomach.

Both security guards were quickly searched and disarmed, their hands quickly tied behind their backs. The two robbers got their guns, while the first and fourth ones converged to the desks.

"Now listen," the first one barked, "I want your vault open right now, with no delay! If it's not open within this very minute, there'll be casualties among your clients as well as among your colleagues! Your choice!"

Charlie was outside, standing not far from the bank. He wasn't wearing his sunglasses any more. He knew what was happening inside, so he didn't feel well at all. He was feeling some guilt for leaving Laura inside when he knew what was going to happen.

Somebody entered the bank, Charlie saw him immediately grabbed. There was nothing he could do.

It was the third robber who grabbed the new-comer and put him down, very brutally, on the floor. "Don't move, stay the fuck down!" he shrieked.

The vault was already open, two of the hooded robbers were taking as much money as they could, putting it in two big bags, while a third one was outside the vault, looking around.

When they finished, the two ones inside the vault ran out of it, as quickly as they could.

There were police sirens sounding in a distance as the three thieves ran to the bank exit with their two filled bags, looking around and shouting 'Stay down!' 'Don't look up!' They joined the fourth one at the entrance door and they all ran out together.

Then some supernatural calm reigned inside. Nothing and nobody was moving. One could hear a fly, even with the remote sounds of the sirens.

Charlie could see the thieves rushing out of the bank, then getting into their car parked right in front of the entrance and abruptly starting it. As it rolled away the car made absolutely no noise except for its tyres screeching like crazy.

He started walking, then running, to the bank entrance. He went inside.

Inside the bank there was still no movement, or almost none. Everybody in front of the desks was still down, but some people were making moves, seeming not to know whether to stand back up or not. Behind the desk, some employees were kind of wandering, under shock.

Charlie looked around, looking for Laura. Finally he spotted her and ran to her. She was still down, lying against the desk.

He touched her, she jumped and looked up.

"Charlie…" she whispered, smiling weakly. Her sunglasses were off as well.

Charlie helped her up. She was the first client to get back on her feet.

Then she turned round… and saw her money on the counter. The robbers hadn't seen it. Apparently they hadn't cared about the cash that was behind the desks. They had showed up late in the day, to be sure to find the vault filled with cash.

Life is always full of surprises.

The teller, who had just stood up, saw the cash too. Laura picked it up but the teller grabbed her wrist right away. She was looking upside down. "What are you doing?" she asked.

"What are *you* doing?" Laura asked, highly surprised. "It's my money."

"In case you didn't notice, we just got robbed," the girl said. Her voice was trembling.

"So what? None of my business. And you have good insurance. Turn me loose!" Laura ordered.

"I can't."

"Let go!"

The teller didn't let go, so Laura started to fight. Progressively the clients were getting back on their feet. And some others were entering the place. The guards didn't stop them from coming in, too shaken themselves to react properly.

"This cash has to stay in here now," the girl was saying.

"What?" Laura fought more to turn loose, the teller kept her grip on her wrist… as they were struggling the teller saw Charlie, standing nearby. And she froze, keeping her grip tight.

"Hey, I know you!" she exclaimed. "I saw you on TV!" Then she looked back at Laura. "I know you too! You're Laura Ingrams!" She started fighting even harder now. "Drop the cash! We need it much more than you do!"

"You're fuckin' crazy!" Laura said, starting to get frantic.

"You're loaded enough!" the girl barked back.

"I just withdrew that cash, let me go!"

"Help!" the girl started calling.

Laura punched her in the face, as hard as she could, to make her shut up. The girl had to release her wrist as she collapsed on the floor behind her desk.

"Let's go!" Laura said to Charlie.

On her way out she stepped on her sunglasses; she looked down, picked them up. They were intact, she put them back on. "Do the same," she added.

Charlie did.

Then they ran to the exit, as the teller stood back up and started yelling again. "She's Laura Ingrams, with that coma kid on TV! Don't let them go!"

Laura and Charlie managed to leave the bank anyway, without a problem. The clients were too shocked to react properly. And those who had just come in had no reason to stop anybody from leaving.

The police sirens got closer and closer. Laura and Charlie were running away from the bank. Soon they turned the first corner and got out of sight.

Then they stopped running, but they kept walking. Laura looked over her shoulder.

"We need a car now," she said, out of breath. She looked at Charlie. "That little cunt's gonna yell about us being in the area, and the whole city will be closed. We need to leave downtown, as soon as possible."

"Too bad you didn't take your car," Charlie said. He was out of breath too.

"We couldn't take it."

She saw a taxi parked not far from them. Some people were standing in front, on the sidewalk, with much luggage.

"Stay here. But keep looking around." She ran to the taxi, reached it but didn't get into it. She only spoke to the driver. "Sorry sir, do you know where the closest car rental company is?" she asked him.

The driver gave her the info. Laura thanked him, she ran back to Charlie and both of them started running again, following the direction that was opposite to the bank, running as far as possible from the robbery scene.

*

Soon Charlie was waiting alone on a sidewalk, against a wall, close to an open gate, for something to happen.

After two minutes that something happened: a rented car stopped beside him. Laura was behind the wheel. "Get in!" she said to him.

Charlie got in the car immediately, taking the passenger's seat, and the car rolled away along the streets.

"Are we leaving the city?" he asked.

"Not yet, Charlie."

"We have to!"

"And where would we be going? We have time anyway, right?"

"We only have until tomorrow. That's not much time," Charlie objected.

"Let me breathe."

"How did you manage to get this car anyway?"

"I was lucky. And the guy was very obliging. He didn't ask any questions, I showed him the money and that was it. It was quick."

"Did he recognize you?"

"He provided the car, and you were not there with me, and I had my sunglasses on all the time, so I guess he didn't."

"You still don't wanna tell me about your husband?" Charlie asked after a short moment.

"I do," Laura said, looking at him with a smile. "He's a philanthropic businessman. He runs a car firm and a foundation. I've been expecting him to call for a while but he must be too busy. He probably believes we're already in a hotel or something. I don't need his help now anyway."

"How long have you been married to him?"

"Three years…" she said.

"I suppose you don't have any kids."

That was not a question but an observation. Laura was not supposed to say anything back, so she stayed quiet. But she stared at Charlie with a slight smile, as she was also looking at the road. This lasted a long moment.

And some thoughts came through her mind, jumbling together.

A few years before, the current government had passed a law, with the aim of controlling and limiting births. A first step to fight overpopulation. It had been decided that each couple would be allowed to have two babies, at the very most. A third newborn was allowed only if the two previous ones were the same gender. If a 'forbidden', 'illegal' baby was conceived, he/she was seized just after birth and placed in foster care, or inside a new kind of institution that was spreading all over the world, a maternity hospital for such 'forbidden' babies considered orphans, waiting for sterile couples – only them – to come and adopt them.

Of course Laura was not barren. Neither was Paul. Who didn't like kids (babies) and want any in his home. She married him anyway – when she knew the way he felt about babies. Since then she had had time to think. So she'd had to find somebody else, but there was no possible way for her to have any sexual relationship and take the risk of getting pregnant when she was still married to Paul.

Charlie's sudden, brutal appearance had turned everything upside down. All the more since Paul became kind of attached to the kid, even when he was still in a coma, even when Paul still didn't know anything about him. 'Dirty monkey,' she thought, but she was still understanding how they were feeling – Paul and also Detective Robredon and Doctor Sanford when they had their conversation about Charlie at the hospital. Charlie was not a baby any more, and if he had lost his memory, she could guess he hadn't lost any of the faculties he had; he could speak very fluently, like any normal person. And as a teenager getting close to adulthood, he wouldn't have to be cared for every day, there wouldn't be any maternal milk to give him, any loud cries to take from him, any diapers to put on him, etc. One could even say that Charlie had been born to this world as a teenager, almost as an adult and, from any couple's point of view, this had nothing but good, attractive points.

But the thing was, Charlie was a very special case and his family had now been identified. Would that stop somebody like Paul?

Laura was still staring at Charlie, seeming to be thinking, when he suddenly broke the silence. "Do you believe me now?" he asked.

"I'll answer that question later, if you don't mind," Laura said. "Now let me drive. We don't need to get pulled over."

Laura kept driving through the immediate suburbs of San Francisco, towards an unknown destination supposed to be a hotel or motel.

Then, all of a sudden, as the car was rolling by a building surrounded by a concrete wall, it turned and entered the place, through an open gate.

"Is it here?" Charlie asked.

Laura didn't answer.

The car rolled through a small tunnel, then emerged in a yard, and stopped.

Charlie looked around. The building was long, surrounding them on all four sides. They were parked in the middle yard. It was not a hotel or a motel, or anything similar.

It was a military building. Barracks.

Charlie saw people in uniforms – soldiers – and he looked at Laura, stunned, his eyes and mouth wide open.

"Don't look at me like that, Charlie," she said peacefully. "I'm doing what I have to do."

"What are you doing?"

"While I was renting this car I made a phone call."

"I…" Charlie was trying to understand.

"The commander of this base is a good friend of my husband's," she explained. "He'll take good care of you here, before he has you evacuated."

"Evacuated?"

"To your home. In Arkansas. As soon as possible. That's what he told me. You belong there, Charlie. With your family. And as a soldier you belong here. In these barracks."

"I'm not a soldier…!" he exclaimed. He could guess he was but he was not ready yet to face it.

"You are, Charlie, but you forgot. You forgot it all. You lost your memory. You forgot all about your past."

"Er…" Charlie didn't expect to be talked to like this. This woman didn't know about him, she didn't know anything, how could she be so sure, only after something she saw on a screen and read in a paper?

"You even forgot your name," she continued. "You forgot your name and you expect people to believe anything you say about the future."

"I don't. The fact is I still can see the future."

"This is too much for them and for me, Charlie."

"And my name's not part of the future."

"Whatever, I can't handle it."

"But you do believe me…"

"Of course I believe you now," she finally admitted. "But who else will?"

"That's why you're leaving me behind," he said.

"I'm not abandoning you, Charlie," she said. "I'm helping you. You'll be better off with these people. Don't be afraid."

"I don't know…" he said, shaking his head, totally lost now. He knew Laura was doing her best to help him. But she didn't know she couldn't help him. Especially by doing this. At such a moment it was impossible for him to think another way.

"There's something you need to know," she announced. "About your parents."

He looked back at her. "My parents? Really?"

"You have the right to know about what your parents did. They expect you to be brought back to them by the army."

"What does that mean?"

"They turned you over to the army. They did it because you voluntarily committed to the army before that tornado took you away. But of course they don't know you forgot everything about this. They don't know you lost your memory. So far nobody does, but me. I didn't tell the commander about it, on the phone. Even my husband doesn't know about it yet. But it's all right." She stopped, took a breath. "Charlie, your parents thought you were dead," she added. "All these years…" She looked around, then: "I'm very sorry, Charlie. I know how hard this whole situation is for you. But there's nothing I can do for you. Except turning you over to the army as well. I'm no family to you. You have no family in this city. The people here can't do anything for you either. All they'll do is keep using you, for their own profit and pleasure."

"But you took me with you anyway."

"Wrong," Laura said, shaking her head. "I only found you on the beach. My husband did take you with him. He made the decision to take you to our house, when you were in the hospital, in a coma. But he's not here now. And he doesn't know about your ability, when I do."

"Did you tell the commander about it, on the phone?" he asked, obviously showing concern.

"No. Of course I didn't. Nobody knows about that either, but me. Don't worry." After a couple of seconds: "Goodbye, Charlie." This was said with a definitive tone. She had nothing more to tell him, and probably didn't want him to say anything more.

They kept looking at each other, Charlie with disbelief, Laura with more and more sorrow.

Until Charlie opened his door and got out of the car.

There were some soldiers in uniforms standing

or walking around in the yard. All looking straight at him. The commander, one of those standing the closest to the car, was among them. He came to him.

"Mister Bradshaw…?" he said.

Charlie nodded with kind of approval. He was still not sure.

"I'm the commander of this base, and believe it or not," he said, holding out a hand, "I'm very happy to make your acquaintance."

Charlie was not sure of this either. He still shook hands with the man. "Thank you," he said.

"Please come with me."

As Charlie started walking away with him, he had a look over his shoulder.

And he caught Laura standing by the car, looking at him walking away. And smiling at him. Charlie kept walking.

IV

They both entered the building. There were other soldiers walking around but they didn't dare disturb somebody walking by the commander. All they could do was stare and speak under their breaths.

"Before you leave this place, young man," the commander said to him, "I'd like you to meet some people who are more than close to me. I told 'em about you coming here as soon as I got the call, and they almost lost their minds. They're burning to meet you in the flesh. Hope you won't mind."

Charlie didn't say anything.

"My office is on the ground floor," the commander added.

They reached the end of the corridor and passed a door, then another one. Then another corridor, smaller, then they reached a closed door.

"Here we are," he said, opening the door. "After you."

He let Charlie go in first, then he entered the room and closed the door.

Two other people were in the room. One man in

the army uniform, one woman, dressed as a civilian. Both sitting.

"Young man," the commander told Charlie as he was walking to his desk, "I'd like you to meet…" He had a seat. "…my Second in Command, and… my wife."

The woman stood up. "I made it here as quickly as I could…!" she said, looking very excited. She walked to Charlie and held out a hand. "I'm so happy to meet you." They shook hands. "I've heard so much about you on TV and in the papers!"

"Thank you, ma'am."

"You can call me Susan," she said.

Her husband looked up at her.

"Very well. Thank you… Susan," Charlie said.

"You're welcome."

The Second in Command stood up and walked to Charlie in his turn. "I'm very proud to meet a real patriot. Especially when he's so young." He held out a hand, Charlie shook it, nodding. He seemed not to know what they were talking about. But they couldn't notice, unaware. "I wish you could stay here, with us," he continued, "but unfortunately that's impossible… you know, I was 17 years and 10 months old, when I joined the US Army in the first place."

Charlie started to say something, but finally he closed his mouth.

"Do you want to say something, my boy?"

"No, sir," Charlie said. "Nothing at all. Except, well… er… congratulations."

"Thank you so much, young man."

"Mister Bradshaw…" the commander said.

"Yes…" Charlie said. Surprised by the use of 'Mister' on him.

"Before you leave, there's something I need to talk with you about… what you said. You know, the earthquake."

"Yes…"

"Did you really mean it?"

"You heard about it?" Charlie asked him.

"Of course, it was on TV."

"Oh. Yes, of course."

"I guess everybody heard it. So? Was it serious?"

Charlie shrugged. "I guess it still is." The emergency of the situation was now lost on him.

"You still mean it?"

"Yes, sir. I still do."

"There's gonna be an earthquake tomorrow, right?" The commander really wanted to be convinced.

"In the morning," Charlie said, very simply.

"Really? In the morning?"

"Yes, in the morning."

"And San Francisco will be destroyed? Like in 1906?"

"Like in 1906," Charlie echoed, with a shrug.

"What makes you so sure?"

"I don't wanna talk about it."

"Okay. You seem to know so much, so what do you suggest?" the commander asked.

The answer to this question was rather obvious. The commander clearly showed his disbelief by asking this. Charlie understood this right away but he showed no reaction.

"Simple. Evacuate the whole barracks," he said. "Everybody here. Not only me."

The commander stood up. "Okay. We'll evacuate you now, and the rest of us later. How's that?" he suggested.

"All right, but don't wait until it happens to do it."

"Let's go now," the commander said. He'd heard enough. He started to walk to the door but his wife stopped him.

"Wait honey," she said. "I've brought my digital camera." Then, to Charlie: "Can we take some photos of us with you? As souvenirs? Please."

"No problem," Charlie said, nodding but looking far away.

"My dear…" the commander said, "we don't have time for that."

Ignoring her husband, Susan walked to her handbag and took a camera out of it.

Then they started taking photos of Charlie surrounded by two people, depending on who was holding the camera.

When the photo show was finished: "Thank you so much, Mister Bradshaw… can I call you Charlie?" Susan asked gently.

"Sure thing, Susan."

She walked quickly to her handbag again and took a pen and a piece of paper out of it. Then she came back to Charlie. "Can I have your autograph… Charlie?" she asked.

Charlie scratched his head, showing sincere embarrassment. "Er... I'm afraid not," he answered, shaking his head. "I'm really sorry."

He had lost everything about himself, including his own signature.

Charlie was surrounded by four young, armed soldiers in uniforms, as they were all marching, in quick time, to seven helicopters lined up, side by side. The commander was walking ahead of them.

They reached the first helicopter and boarded it. Two of the soldiers got in the cockpit, the two others in the back, along with Charlie. The commander stayed out.

"Have a good trip home, young man," he said. "It's been a pleasure."

Charlie was not convinced by this, but still: "Thanks, sir, but..."

"But what?"

Charlie thought it'd be better to keep silent for a short moment. "This helicopter won't start," he announced peacefully.

"What?" This came from the first soldier, not believing of course.

"What are you talking about?" the commander asked.

"It won't fly," Charlie said.

"Hey... please." This came from the second soldier, a black one.

"I mean it," Charlie said.

"You mean you're crazy," the first soldier said.

"What do you think, that this chopper is a plastic toy or what?"

"You tell me, I don't know," Charlie retorted. "All I know is, we ain't going anywhere."

"You better stop drinking."

"I don't drink."

"Okay, so leave the school yard and quit Play Station."

"Play what?"

Then came the voice of one of the two other soldiers, from the cockpit: "Hey guys!"

"What?" the commander asked.

"We've got a situation here…"

"What situation?" The commander walked to the cockpit door, which was still open. "What's going on?"

The third and fourth soldiers were trying to start the chopper. They were trained, expert copter pilots.

"Seems to be a problem, sir," the fourth soldier said.

"What's the problem?"

"We actually don't know, sir. Er… well, we don't know. The engine, the rotor, the starter… nothing is actually working, sir."

"Are you pulling my leg?"

"With all due respect, sir," the third soldier said, "I'd like to, but… I'm not."

"Me neither, sir," the fourth soldier said.

As they were speaking they were still trying to start the helicopter. Which was staying dumb.

"I don't understand," the fourth soldier said, shaking his head, his face starting to sweat.

The two other soldiers were just behind them, watching.

"Are you sure you didn't forget anything?" the second soldier asked.

"If you think so you can take my seat," the third soldier retorted rather harshly.

"No thanks…" The second soldier moved to the back. And faced Charlie. And froze, starting to stare at him. And moved back forwards, to the cockpit. Charlie himself was dazed. "Guys, you better start this damned chopper," the soldier said quickly, "I'm starting to get the creeps."

"What the hell d'you think we're trying to do?" the fourth soldier asked, exasperated.

The commander lost it: "Don't try," he suddenly yelled, "just start the fuckin' copter!"

*

Charlie was back inside the building, alone in some room. He hadn't been evacuated – the attempt had failed.

It was a very classical room, for one person, with a single set up bed, a table, a chair, a closet and a TV set laying on some small piece of furniture. Charlie was sitting on the chair, against the wall opposite from the table. He was waiting.

After a short time the door opened and the commander came in. Charlie stood up.

"Stay seated," the commander said, smiling. As

Charlie was sitting back down: "You should be lying down."

"Why, sir?" Charlie asked.

"You just should. So you're ready when at least one of the choppers is fixed."

"I woke up from a coma today. I'm all right."

"Oh yes, I forgot that detail." The commander leaned against the door he had just closed. "Well kid, you've signed your entrance here."

"I didn't do anything."

"I know that. I'm not trying to make you responsible for anything. But this base was built rather recently, and I guess what's happening now is good advertising for us." He grinned a little.

"You mean all the choppers are down?"

"Yes. All of them. They've been sabotaged," the commander announced very seriously. "Whoever did this I can't figure out how he or they could do it so quickly. Something else. There's been a leak."

"A leak?" Charlie was way behind everything now. He wasn't getting any of what was happening.

"Possibly more than one. About you being here. Except that woman, nobody outside was supposed to know."

"Outside?"

"We're under siege, Charlie. I'm sorry."

Many people were already standing all around the barracks, mainly in front of the entrance door, making a lot of noise.

"It didn't take long," the commander added. He

was looking really concerned about this new, extraordinary situation.

"Laura…"

"No," the commander said, shaking his head. "There's no point in her doing that after calling me about you and bringing you here."

"Then who?"

"I guess it's my fault. I should have had you evacuated right away. But I have waited. And I've made some calls myself." The commander paused. "I suppose that's the reason for the choppers being sabotaged."

"You mean…"

"My deputies, and my own wife, yes, maybe. Even if I can't tell for sure."

"Where are they?"

"My deputies are in my office. My wife is on her way home, but I still can't reach her on the phone."

"And…" There was nobody around Charlie could trust. Not even here. Laura was wrong.

"Now you need to know, Charlie, this is a US Air Force base. Everyone in here has a pilot's license. It means that anyone here could have sabotaged the copters. Anyone."

"Including…" Charlie was hesitating, "including yourself?"

"Yes, Charlie," the commander nodded. "Including myself. But believe me, young man, if it was me, I'd have let in all those crazies outside a while ago, and you'd already be walking along the streets, with some big cross on your shoulder. Don't you agree?"

"I suppose so, yes."

"You know what I'm talking about, right?"

"I do," Charlie answered. "Laura told me already."

"Aren't you afraid about it?" the commander asked him.

"Should I be?"

"You should. You still haven't seen those people outside. Most of them are religious lunatics. And they're after you."

"I know," Charlie said.

"Now, about that earthquake…"

"Yes?"

"You're still serious about it?" the commander asked, more seriously than he did before. Things had changed.

"I don't wanna talk about it," Charlie said again.

"Look, you knew that the choppers wouldn't start…"

"I did, yes."

"And you told us…"

"I only wanted to make myself useful."

"…but maybe you should have kept your mouth shut," the commander finished.

"I know. That's what I'll do, starting now," Charlie said.

"But you can talk to me, Charlie. I'm kind of forced to believe you now."

"I won't say anything else."

"D'you still think I should have the barracks evacuated as soon as possible?"

"It's up to you."

"Who are you, Charlie?"

"I'd like to know. I guess you know more about me than I know about myself."

"All right. You stay here until one of our choppers is fixed, or until the police send us one of theirs. In the meanwhile I'll try to find out who sabotaged the helicopters and who made the calls. Is that a deal?" the commander proposed.

"I guess so," Charlie said.

"One last thing. Today is my daughter's birthday."

"Really?"

"Yes…"

"How old is she?" Charlie asked.

"17. Would you like to meet her?" the commander suggested.

"It'd be a pleasure. Yes," Charlie agreed.

"Great. She'd really like to make your acquaintance as well."

"Sure thing."

"We intend to celebrate it here, in the barracks."

"In here…?"

"First in here, yes."

"At what time?"

"Starting at 8. It's now around 6.30."

"All right."

The commander stepped away from the door. "The door is reinforced," he said. "So are the windows. Don't try to open them. There is air-conditioning but you won't need it. Do you hear it?"

"Yes."

"I'll come back for you, so please don't panic. And watch some TV, you may hear some more about yourself."

The commander started to leave, then he stopped and turned back to Charlie, hesitating. Then he went to him, taking something out of one of his pockets.

"Take this," he said, handing it to Charlie. It was a key. Charlie took it. "The key for the door. Just in case." Then the commander left, closing the door behind him.

Charlie stood up, walked to the small, old-fashioned TV set, and turned it on. And he heard about himself right away.

He first saw people yelling outside the barracks. Most of them were shouting his name. At that moment it was too early to know if they were meaning to help or harm.

The TV camera and image travelled across the roaring crowd for a moment, before keeping steady in front of a female TV reporter.

"We're in front of a US Air Force base in the suburbs of San Francisco and people are still gathering fast," she announced. "We can estimate their number at two thousand, all cheering for or against one person, that young boy named Charlie Bradshaw."

Paul and Laura were sitting in front of their TV screen, watching too. In their house, the real one. There was nobody left around it now, the protest – if there still was one – had moved to another place.

"According to an unknown source, he was brought into the barracks by Mister Ingrams' wife with the intention to have the boy evacuated very quickly, but apparently it failed, for a reason that is unknown as well."

"Some great work you did," Paul said. He was upset but not mad. He knew his wife by heart, there was no way she ever could do anything that serious without some good reason.

"They were supposed to evacuate him at once!" she complained.

"Well, they failed."

"I can see that."

"Why didn't you call me before just... giving him to them?"

"I gave him to them, that's all. I made the decision myself."

"Bad decision."

"No. Good decision," she retorted, defending herself.

"Tell me more."

"Look," she said, pointing at the TV screen.

The news was now about the bank robbery that had occurred downtown about an hour before.

Charlie opened the closet. There was a military uniform inside. Only one. On a hanger.

"...there are reports of Laura Ingrams and young Charlie having been seen at the scene of a bank robbery this afternoon..."

As he turned to the screen he took the hanger out.

"A bank robbery…" Paul almost whispered. He turned to Laura. "And both of you were there?" he asked.

"Yes. I was there, inside the bank, with Charlie. We got in there before it happened and guess what… Charlie told me," she said heavily. "He told me it was going to happen. As soon as we got inside he told me. He knew."

"He *knew?*" Paul was dumbfounded.

"Yes. I swear to God."

"Did you believe him?"

"I admit I didn't. Until it did happen."

"And…?"

"It went fast. In only a few minutes the robbers were already out, with what they came for. I could run out with him before the police showed up. But after that I had to think." She paused. "Look, Paul… he's a *precog.*"

"A what?"

"A precognitive. Precog. He's able to see into the future."

"Oh… he can see into the future, huh?" he said.

"I know it sounds crazy but… look, I saw it working, all right? Please believe me, don't treat me like an escapee from some mental place."

She preferred not to tell him that the kid had lost his memory as well, that he forgot everything about his past. It could be too much to take for him in a couple of minutes.

"Don't worry," he said, unconvincingly. "So you

knew that… and you turned him over to the army?" Paul asked, unable to hide his bad surprise.

"The army doesn't know," Laura explained. "The idea was that they evacuate him as quickly as possible, before they could know."

"Maybe they know now. Maybe they've known since Charlie came out of coma and talked about that coming earthquake."

"They couldn't be sure after that."

"They probably are now," Paul said, on the alert. "Charlie is still here, they've kept him with them!"

Laura stood up and leant toward her husband, kind of angry. "Now listen, the commander of that base is a good friend of yours, right? Why don't you call him and ask about what happened?"

There was a beat as Paul stared at her, stunned. Laura went on, lowering her voice, stepping backwards. "Look, I'm sorry, okay? But you're talking about your own friend, so Charlie is safer than you think!"

Paul sighed deeply. "Laura… there are lunatic people everywhere," he said. "Even in the army. Maybe, especially in the army. Who knows, maybe my commanding friend is a religious nut, or a war crazy, who's hidden his real nature until now. Everybody has a hidden face."

"Okay look, I'd just realized that Charlie didn't belong here. All right?" she said, articulating each letter and word very clearly. "He had to be brought back to his folks. I know I'm right. You know it too. If Charlie is still over there it's not my fault."

"Maybe you could have called me about what

happened at the bank. So we could evacuate him ourselves."

"Well, I didn't call you," she said. "I called your army friend. He's got what is required for an evacuation. You don't."

"All right, don't get upset." There was a moment of silence as he was thinking. "If that boy is really a precog…"

"He is, trust me on this."

"…and if he meant what he said," he continued, "then the city has to be evacuated today."

"You really think this whole city can be evacuated within the next twelve or eighteen hours?"

"I don't think so, I'm just saying it."

"And what d'you plan to do about it?"

"I can call a press conference."

"Come on. Come on! They won't listen," she said, with good certitude, "they'll never believe you without some good evidence. They will laugh at you. I know what I'm talking about, I didn't believe it myself. May God forgive me, I almost laughed at the boy."

"You're not everybody," he retorted.

"And if they do believe you you'll do nothing else but start some big panic. Forget it."

"Better some big panic than nothing at all."

"What about the boy?"

"I'll tell you what's gonna happen. I'll call a press conference. You'll go back for the boy. And we'll evacuate him ourselves."

"Paul, you have to believe me," Laura said, searching for his support, realizing that it was important now. "I did it... for his own protection."

"I know, my dear," he said. "I believe you."

v

Charlie closed the closet. He had finished with the green, complete US Air Force uniform which was on him now, the hat included.

He walked to a sink and looked at himself in a mirror above it.

Then he walked to the door, used the key to unlock it, opened it and left the room, closing the door behind him.

He ended up in an empty corridor that stretched along both sides of him, with the left one ending about ten yards ahead, and opened to another corridor that extended again, to both sides. The right side was a dead end, with a door at the end. He walked along the left side.

He reached the end of the corridor and had a look on both sides. Nobody, nothing, no noise.

He turned left. The corridor on this side was much longer than on the other. He finally changed his mind and turned back, heading right. And reached the end of the corridor. He had a look on the left side.

Nobody, nothing. And the corridor was very long. But it was empty. And silent. Almost silent.

He could hear some noise, screams coming from the outside.

He started walking, then running along the empty corridor. Running because in the end he was almost wishing to come across somebody, even if he didn't really want to.

He ran, reaching the end of the long corridor… and saw nobody. Only a wall with many closed wooden doors, all along both sides of the left corridor. On the right were more doors but no corridor.

Where were all of them? What was going on?

Suddenly there was a ring. Coming from inside his uniform. A cell phone ring.

He leaped up like a kangaroo and searched himself, frantically. He finally took out a device, a tiny cell phone, ringing loudly. There was a call, from somebody. Unknown number. He refused to take it, and the noise stopped.

But he didn't know what to do with the device.

The phone sounded again. Another call. Same one? Same person? The number was still unknown.

He took the risk, and the call. He put the device up to his ear, with a shaky hand.

"Hello?" a voice said.

Charlie didn't answer.

"Charlie?"

"So… sorry?" Charlie said, with huge amazement.

"Charlie?" the voice said again.

"Who is this?" Charlie asked, trembling a little.

"Charlie, is that you?"

"Who's speaking?"

"It's the commander, who do you think?"

Charlie was astounded. "Commander?"

"Yes. You took this call rather quickly."

"Mister…"

"I knew you'd put on the uniform. That was a little test on you. Where are you now? Don't lie to me."

"Well… er…"

"You walked out of the room, right?"

"But… how can you know?"

"I run the place, Charlie. Now follow my advice, go back to your room and don't leave again."

"I can't," Charlie said.

"Charlie, listen. I've convened everybody in the TV room."

"The TV room?"

"They're all talking about you on TV. So I've sent everybody to that room, so they just keep watching. I thought this way I could isolate the saboteurs and spot them."

"The corridors are empty!" Charlie said.

"Maybe not. If you see or hear anybody, don't cross them, don't even go to them. Because they are probably after you."

"They?"

"Of course. How d'you think all the choppers went down so quickly?"

"Where are you now?" Charlie asked.

"I'm in my office. Alone. But I just came back in, after I saw you walking along."

"You saw me…"

"Of course. Now get back to your room."

"If I go to my room they may see me."

"Get back now, the sooner you do it, the better it will be."

Then Charlie heard the dial tone. The commander had hung up. Charlie put the cell phone away.

He looked around. Still nobody to be seen. All of them in the TV room but…

He started walking again, the reverse way, and reached the long corridor, having to cross it again.

He did it, running fast. He reached the end of it and had a look to the right. Nobody.

So he took the corridor, walking slowly, reaching the one leading to his door and bedroom. He stopped, had a look.

There were two people in uniforms, in front of the door. They were not trying to open it; they were just listening, trying to hear any noise coming from the inside.

He pulled back, quickly, gasping slightly. How did they know the exact door? Maybe it was the only room with a reinforced door. Maybe not…

He had another look. One of the two guys had his back to him, hiding the other one. Charlie pressed his luck, and went quickly from the corridor end to the other one.

The two guys heard the move, they turned their heads to its source but they didn't see him. They didn't have time to see anything or anybody.

Charlie reached the end of the long corridor and had a look. And he saw some other guys in uniforms. Three guys, standing still. Seeming to be talking something over.

He pulled back. And looked behind him. The corridor was still empty. He heard the voices of the guys in the other corridor.

He reached the end and had another look. The two guys were still in the same position, but one of them was trying to force the door open.

Then there was the noise. A noise that was always growing louder. Coming from above. From some helicopter, sounding to come right to the barracks.

After a short moment Charlie moved back to the other end of the corridor and had a new look.

The three guys were gone. The long corridor was now empty.

As the noise kept growing, Charlie, instinctively, had a look behind him. Just to make sure he was alone.

And he saw the two guys, standing still around the corner, looking straight at him, saying nothing.

A police helicopter was approaching the building. Inside the copter were three men, the pilot, the co-pilot and a policeman, who was using a radio.

"…Yes, we're approaching," the police officer said into the radio. "We will be landing in a few minutes. How's the kid? Over."

Charlie managed to turn the corner and to start

walking the long corridor, trying to look innocent, but the two soldiers followed him after a shortly exchanged look.

After a few seconds he had a brief look over his shoulder. The two were still following. They were looking calm, maybe trying to figure out if the boy was the one they were looking for.

Then there was a ring. The same one, from the cell phone. Charlie took it out and pressed the green button, but as he was about to speak the two guys grabbed him from behind, trying to cover the phone with their hands as well as Charlie's mouth.

The commander was still in his office, behind his desk, speaking into his cell phone.

"Charlie? ... Charlie?" he called.

Charlie fought to say something in the phone, which was hard, almost mission impossible. The two guys were doing whatever it took to keep him silent, and to take the cell phone away from him. They tried to drag him down on the floor when Charlie was struggling to stay standing.

Charlie managed to step on one of the guys' foot, as hard as he could, and the guy released his pressure on the phone. Then Charlie bit the hand that was covering his mouth. The hand was removed.

"Commander...?" Charlie managed to say.

The two guys silenced him again, at once.

"Charlie?" the commander called again. He was

hearing distant sounds. Sounds of fight. "Shit!" he cursed, suddenly enraged. He had just understood what was happening.

He hung up and, as he was walking to the door, he dialled another number and put the phone back up to his ear. "I'll need you out of the room, right now..." he said quickly.

He left the office, almost running. Just as he did he could hear the sounds. He moved along the corridors, quietly, carefully, and as quickly as possible, holding up a gun in his right hand and keeping his cell phone in his left hand.

As he kept moving the noises got closer... he finally turned a corner and saw two guys in military uniforms, holding a third one who was struggling and groaning on the floor.

The commander pocketed his cell phone and moved quickly to them, his gun pointed.

The two soldiers were smothering Charlie to keep him from screaming, while trying to control him, to make him motionless. "Let it go!" one of them said.

Charlie, of course, didn't let it go, struggling to turn loose.

"Stop it!" the other one said to him, gasping. "We're not gonna hurt you!"

"You bet you're not gonna hurt him!" the commander barked. His gun was put to the second soldier's head. The two soldiers froze, still holding Charlie tight. Both of them still couldn't see the commander but they knew his voice.

"Let the kid go!" the commander ordered.

"Commander…" the first soldier said.

"Exactly! Do as I say, now! Get away from him!"

"Shit…" the first soldier sighed.

The commander grabbed him, trying to throw him away from Charlie, but the soldier was keeping his grip on the boy. "Turn him loose!" the commander said.

Suddenly, gunshots were heard from a distance. The commander looked up.

The police chopper was getting hit by a series of bullets shot from nowhere.

"What the hell is going on?" the pilot said, shocked.

"Somebody is shooting at us!" the policeman said. He couldn't see where the shots were coming from but he had enough experience to figure it out immediately.

The shooting continued until the chopper had to turn and fly back.

"Mayday, mayday!" the co-pilot said in his radio. "We're getting shot!"

On the streets the people around the base were all looking up, watching the copter in trouble like it was some kind of a show. Screaming and cheering and gasping, as the chopper was struggling to fly back to where it came from.

The commander looked back down. The two guys had turned to him during the gunfire from the outside. "One more time, release the kid," he said again. He couldn't stand to be forced to say the same thing many times, and was fighting to keep control of himself.

"No way," the first soldier said.

"You're under my command, you do as I say."

"Not this time, commander," the second soldier said, shaking his head.

Both guys were still lying on the floor, yet they were talking like this to their commander, who had a gun on them from above; a surrealistic scene.

"What the hell does that mean?" the commander said, disconcerted and angry for being so.

"We're under your command, it doesn't mean you shoot anyone not following your orders," the second soldier said.

"Are you gonna shoot us, commander?"

They were challenging him now.

"Enough of that shit," the commander said. "On your feet."

Both guys stood up, forcing Charlie to do the same, still holding him tight, using him as a protection hostage, a shield.

"And for the last time, let him go!"

The second soldier held on. "No."

"We're taking him out with us," the first soldier said. "And you won't stop us."

"*What??*" The commander couldn't believe his ears. "What do you think I'm doing?"

"You can't stop us," the second soldier said.

"Don't force me to shoot."

"D'you know who this kid is?" the first soldier asked.

"You mean who you believe he is."

"He's sent by God!" the second soldier said.

"No! He is His son himself!" the first one said. "He's Jesus! Jesus Christ!" He was almost crying.

The commander shook his head with sadness. "And you're out of my command. You will go home after I finish with you. I mean, you'll be on your way to the closest mental hospital. I don't want any fanatics in my base."

"You don't understand," the first one insisted. "He *is* Jesus. In the flesh."

"Stop that shit!" the second one retorted with brutality. "He's only God's messenger."

"He's the Christ," the first one said, ignoring. "Resurrected. Or reincarnated. Whatever. He's just too young to realize. He needs to be told everything."

The commander couldn't keep a slight smile from appearing on his face. Despite the difficulty of his situation he was finding kind of funny to see two fanatics contradicting themselves in front of him.

"Bullshit!" he said. "He's just a kid. But both of you are too crazy to realize."

"No matter what you think," the second soldier said. "We're taking him out. He doesn't belong in this place."

"Neither do you."

"We'll be back," the first one followed. "God's will."

"Where are you taking him? To some church?" As the two crazies said nothing, the commander turned to Charlie. "What d'you think of this, Charlie?"

"Don't you call him Charlie!" the first one shrieked. "His name is Jesus Christ! Show him some respect!" He was crying now.

"Commander...!" Charlie suddenly yelled. But it was too late.

The three other soldiers Charlie saw before, also in their uniforms, appeared quickly behind the commander, their guns pointed at his head. They had come down from the upper floor and had heard what was happening downstairs.

"Freeze, commander," the third soldier said, softly.

"Drop your gun," the fourth one said. "Now."

Charlie had just spotted them when he'd yelled.

The commander froze, but he didn't drop his gun.

"I said, drop the gun!" the fourth one repeated.

"If I were you I'd comply," the first one said to the commander.

"Are you gonna shoot me if I don't?" the commander said, keeping his gun pointed, trying to buy some time. "Don't get confused, I'm not under your command. You are under mine."

"Yeah, but we have guns on your head," the third one said. "Drop yours. Now."

"You don't want the kid hurt."

"That's right," the fifth one approved. "You're in charge here, but you know what? We don't give a shit about you. We want the kid. Unhurt, yes, of course. Alive and in good health."

"So what are you waiting for? Shoot me." It was the commander's turn for the challenging.

"God doesn't allow killing," the third one disagreed.

"Oh yes. I forgot. So you can't make me drop my gun," the commander logically concluded.

"Unless…" the fifth one said.

Instead of finishing his sentence he started to raise his hand in the air, about to knock the commander down with his gun. Right at that moment… *he* was the one who went down, knocked from behind by…

…one of the two commander's deputies.

"Don't move!" the other deputy said, appearing behind him. "Both of you!"

Both deputies had their guns pointed at the two other guys with guns, from behind.

"Now you both get down on the floor or you can say goodbye to your heads," the first deputy said.

The two armed guys dropped their guns.

"Same for you," the commander said to the two others, "and release the kid, goddammit!"

*

The policeman in the helicopter was desperately trying to get the barracks' commander on his radio. "Hello, commander, hello? Hello?" he was repeating. "Do you copy? Over."

The commander came back into his office, followed by his deputies and Charlie. He rushed to the radio and picked up the receiver. "Yeah?" he said. "Over."

"Commander? Over."

"Yes! Over!"

"We've been shot at," the police officer announced. "Over."

"Sorry? Over."

"Somebody's shot at us so we couldn't land! We're on our way back. Over."

The commander clinched his teeth and closed his fists. "Shit!" he barked. "Look, you've got to come back to us. Over."

"Are you kidding? The copter is wasted. We'll be lucky if we don't crash and get wasted as well. What's on your side? Over."

"We've encountered some trouble too. You don't want to know. But the kid is all right. We'll talk later. Good luck. Tell your guys to send another copter if possible, we have the situation under control now. Over."

"You mean that…"

"The shooting came from the base," the commander said, with no hesitation. "Let's keep this between us, right? Don't tell anyone, especially the press. Over and out." He cut, and nodded at his two deputies. "Okay, you can evacuate the TV room now."

The deputies nodded and left the office, saying nothing.

Then the commander turned his head to Charlie. "I'm afraid you'll have to stay here for a while longer," he said.

"What happened?" Charlie asked.

"Don't play with me," the commander said, unhappily. "You know what. That's why you left your room, right?"

"Basically, yes," Charlie admitted after a short moment. "I knew there would be some shooting, but that's all."

"Really? What about the kidnapping attempt on yourself? Did you see it happening?" Charlie shrugged a response looking like a very vague yes. "I bet you did," the commander groaned.

"I had to check all this out," Charlie said.

"All right," the commander said. He walked to Charlie and, silently, with a hand gesture, told him to give him something.

Charlie got it. He took the key for his room door out of his pocket and gave it to him, saying nothing more.

"Let's go back," the commander said. "And once you're back in there, find something to do and stick to it. Try the television."

VI

The crowd was always growing bigger and noisier. Keeping yelling, cheering, singing, cursing. Some of the people were holding bibles, or carrying more or less big crosses on their shoulders, or holding signs with 'HAIL JESUS' or 'HE'S BACK' or 'PRAISE THE LORD' or 'JUDGEMENT DAY IS DUE TOMORROW' on them. Some others were holding signs with 'SAVE CHARLIE' or 'STOP ALL WARS' or 'CHARLIE IS NO WEAPON' on them. Anti-war people, who were convinced of Charlie's abilities and didn't want him to be used as a war weapon.

There were also some Satanists who seemed and looked to want the boy burned to death, because he *was* Jesus Christ, the opponent of their God, Satan. Holding signs with 'BURN JESUS', or 'HAIL SATAN', or 'NOT OUR GOD', or 'DELIVER US FROM GOOD' on them. As well as a few small groups of Dalai Lama and Krishna worshippers, singing and drumming noisily while distributing flyers and booklets around. The rest of

173

the crowd was composed of reporters, of curious onlookers, and of more or less well-known, believing showmen, using their mouths and their experience on stage to give as much sales talk as possible to bunches of people gathered around them.

Laura was in the crowd. She was wearing the same sunglasses. She was trying to walk through, but it was difficult, the crowd was now packed. Most of the people around her were screaming and singing, raising their hands in the air. The noise was deafening.

On her way she crossed several leafleters, trying to give out flyers, booklets and magazine issues about all kinds of churches and religious cults. She was always declining them, saying 'No thank you'.

Or almost always.

One of them leafleters happened to be an old man dressed up as a priest and holding a small basket, as if he was in a church, asking for donations he'd give to his lord and master. "For Jesus! Give to Jesus, brothers and sisters! Give to the Lord!" he was saying.

Laura stopped by him and looked down at the basket. It was already filled with coins and bills. This one had found some good business.

The Lord didn't need any money though.

"Give, my sister! Give to the Holy Christ who's back!" he said, this time straight to her.

Laura walked by him, giving nothing.

"Jesus cares, my sister!" he called. "But you

don't seem to care about Him! God bless you anyway!"

Laura kept walking, not listening. A younger man stopped her, holding out a big leaflet. Actually a journal.

"The Paper of Christ! Free! The Paper of Christ!" he was yelling. As Laura took it: "Thank you. God bless you, miss!" He picked up another issue and raised it in the air, as Laura was walking away. "The Paper of Christ..."

Laura kept walking, trying to open the paper. The front of it was showing the body of an adult, crucified on a golden cross. But the head was Charlie's. The drawing was very realistic.

She dropped it right away, with an angry groan.

One of the next encounters was with a young woman with weird eyes. She was holding out two papers. One was an issue of an anti-war magazine. The other one was an anti-Satan magazine.

"He's a child, an innocent creature, prisoner of the Devil and His evil pupils!" the woman was yelling to the crowd. "Join us, and together we'll bring him out of there!"

Laura took the anti-war issue only. Immediately the woman tried to lead her to the group she was part of. "This way, lady," she said, raising a finger. "You must join us!"

But Laura walked away, taking another direction. As she kept walking she was passing even more leafleters promoting the cults they were working for. One of these people was a priest in civilian clothes, who was certain that the child in the barracks was not Jesus. Laura heard what he was saying and stopped.

"He's not the Holy Spirit, God told me he's not!" he said. "He told me to tell everybody, but nobody listens! I'm a priest, somebody listen to me…"

Guffawing a little, Laura took his leaflet. "Relax, Father," she said. "I believe you."

"God bless you, lady," the civilian priest said, grateful. "Jesus loves you!"

Laura kept walking, smiling.

After a little while a young man with brown hair, moustache and beard, wearing only a white sheet around his hips, his both arms half-raised like he was on a cross, walked to her.

"Mother…" he said to her. Then he fell down on her, hugging her hard.

"Hey…!" was the only thing she could say, too stunned to find more.

"Please mother…" the guy moaned, "don't let them kill me!"

"Let go!" Laura ordered loudly.

The young man obeyed right away, stepping back. Then he started laughing, along with some people around.

Laura got it at once. A joke. "Very funny," she said.

She walked away from them, quickly, moving to the sidewalk side, opposite to the barracks. She took out her cell phone.

She ended up close to an itinerant sandwich maker. "Hello lady, are you hungry?" he asked.

"No thank you," Laura said automatically.

"Jesus is back among us, don't you wanna celebrate? Here." He handed her a fresh hot-dog.

"I just said I'm not hungry."

"It's free, come on! Today, no price, no charge!" Laura finally took the sandwich. "God bless you, lady!" he said, gratefully.

"Yeah," she said back, nodding. As she started dialling a number on her cell phone she bit into the sandwich. Almost immediately she spat the mouthful out.

She examined the inside of the hot-dog, and turned to the sandwich maker. "Your sausage is raw!" she said.

"Of course!" he said. "Don't you get it? The Lord is back, we're back to Year Zero! No way to grill any meat now!"

She walked away, shaking her head, and stepped on the sidewalk, the raw hot-dog still in her other hand.

She walked on the sidewalk to a garbage bin, and threw the raw sausage sandwich, the anti-war magazine and the leaflet into it. Then she restarted dialling a number on her cell phone and put the device up to her ear.

"Commander...?" she said.

The commander was able to hear the heavy background noise on the phone. "Laura? Are you outside?"

"What happened with the kid?"

"There's been a few incidents," was all he could

say. And it was enough. Laura got it and didn't show any interest in the details.

"Is he okay?" she only asked.

"Yes, he is. What are you doing outside?"

"What do you think?"

"You know it's impossible," the commander said.

"You know how it is out here. They've all gone nuts already. Sooner or later they'll break in. You have to find a way."

"There's no way."

"Find one. Are you watching TV?" she asked.

Paul arrived from his offices at the main entrance of the building, awaited by a whole pack of reporters with their TV cameras and microphones. Asking a thousand questions at the same time, just as usual.

"We all know where the kid is," he said to them, "so I guess we aren't at the right place."

Another series of mixed questions. Paul could answer one of them only. "No, I don't have any answer to give, since I didn't hear any question clearly. But I can tell you this, I won't give any confirmation about what the boy more or less publicly said about an eventual earthquake that is supposed to occur tomorrow morning."

Charlie was back in the bedroom, watching TV and listening. And seeing Laura's husband for the first time.

"It's up to all of us," Paul was saying. "But whatever we may believe about this thing, we can't just stay here, doing nothing, only waiting for some-body or something or the nature or some miracle, or God, to stop things from happening or to rescue us. We're all on our own. That's all I have to say."

One reporter made himself clearly heard. "Do you believe in fate, sir?" he asked.

"Who doesn't?"

Charlie saw him ignoring the next series of mixed questions that included 'Do you think this Charlie Bradshaw is the Lord Himself?' and 'Do you believe in divine reincarnation or resurrection?' and moving away.

*

The room was in a total darkness. A cake with lighted candles moved through the dark, with people singing 'Happy Birthday to you!'

The cake was put on an invisible table and as soon as the song was over somebody blew out the candles, using his/her breath. Then the darkness resumed as the applause started.

"Okay, turn the lights back on!" a male voice said loudly.

But the lights stayed off.

"Lights back on please!" another voice shouted.

"Thank you in advance," a third one said.

The lights still stayed off.

"What the hell...?" the first voice said, incre-dulously.

Something strange was going on. There was no

179

power outage at the base so somebody must have been playing. Maybe that was part of a birthday trick.

The noise grew louder as the darkness remained, with people groaning, hitting themselves or falling down.

Finally the lights were turned on again, showing only soldiers, the ones standing, the others lying on the floor and quickly standing back up. The room was in more or less disorder. But what was first visible was the invisibility of the main guest: the commander's daughter. Who was supposed to begin the celebration of her birthday in this room. The cake, which was very big, was there, on the table, but a small part of it was missing as well, it had already been cut off. The seventeen blown out candles were on the rest of it.

"Where the fuck is she, man?" a soldier asked himself.

She was in a corridor, walking through it, holding a small plate with a double slice of cake on it. Her name was Isabel. A beautiful young girl with thick, light brown hair. She was showing a great smile.

As she was walking, Charlie and the commander were walking towards her and they finally met.

Isabel's attention was focused on Charlie. "Hi Dad…" she said anyway.

"Hi darling. Let me introduce you to…"

"Everybody knows his name," she interrupted.

'Everybody but me,' Charlie said to himself.

"Yeah," the commander said. "Charlie Bradshaw."

"Exactly."

"Jesus…" the commander started, then he guffawed. "…er, Charlie, sorry."

"This is not funny, Dad," she said.

"…this is Isabel, my daughter."

Isabel held out a hand. "Hello, Charlie…"

"Hi, Isabel," Charlie said, his face expressionless. He was a bit tired from all those introductions. He shook hands with her.

"I've heard so much about you," she said.

'Like everybody else,' Charlie thought. He hadn't done anything special for that though. "You're 17 today, right?" he asked her.

"Yes."

"Well, congratulations. And happy birthday."

"Thank you. How old are you?"

The commander interrupted. "Take him to your private place, okay?" he said to her. "You two will be better off there."

"Sure, Dad. Thank you."

"I have to go get my slice," he said to her. Then, to Charlie. "Keep an eye on her, okay, son?"

"Daddy!"

"I will," Charlie said.

The commander nodded and walked away.

"Don't pay attention to him," she said.

"You're asking a lot here."

"Why?"

"He runs this place. And I'm kind of part of this brigade force."

"Whatever. Do you like cake?" she asked.

"Sure," Charlie said.

"This is a double slice. I sliced it even before the celebration started."

"For the two of us?"

"Sure. Have one."

"Not now."

"Of course not. Come on." She started walking, he followed.

Laura was still outside. The crowd was as noisy as it was before. Maybe more.

Inside the place a door in a wall opened and Charlie and Isabel appeared, slowly.

"Nice cake," Charlie said, licking his fingers.

"Wasn't it?" She looked around. So did he.

"I thought we were going to your place..." he said, surprised to be outside when he thought he'd see and end up in some private room or apartment.

"We are."

There was nobody in the back courtyard. She licked her fingers in her turn and grabbed Charlie's arm. "Come on," she said. She took him to a manhole cover outside. Then she released him and crouched by the cover. "Help me."

"What's this?" he asked, totally disconcerted.

"My private place is outside," she explained. "Outside the base. I'm taking you there."

"Wait a minute..."

"We can't wait. Charlie, this place is under siege.

Don't tell me you wanna stay inside a place that is under siege?"

Charlie hesitated. He didn't know her, after all. She was the daughter of the commander, of somebody who could be trusted, so what? That didn't mean she could be trusted as well.

He had a look around. Still nobody.

"Come on, help me!" Isabel said, insistently.

Charlie finally crouched in his turn and helped her to move the cover off the hole.

"Okay," she said. "You first."

He went down first, then she followed and they closed the opening from below.

*

Among the many people outside were Stuart and the young girl who'd heard something falling down into the sea from the sky. Dan, the boy who was with her on the yacht, was not there – they had broken up. The sun was gone, but she was still wearing her sunglasses. So she had even less chances to spot anybody special in the crowd. She never would.

Stuart took out his cell phone and started dialling a number.

Despite the noise Laura heard the sound from her phone, she took it out, saw the number on it, recognized Stuart's.

She hesitated, finally she let the ringing go on, not taking the call, letting her voicemail take over.

Isabel and Charlie were running in the sewers, Isabel using a torch to light this new totally dark place.

"It's okay," she said, "you can run with no fear. These sewers are very neat, the soldiers clean it up themselves, regularly, just in case. So they can always use them with no problem."

"I see."

At a moment Isabel stopped. "This way."

They turned and followed a smaller path, walking this time.

Finally they came to a ladder.

"It's here," she announced. "Our way out."

Charlie climbed first. After about a minute he reached the cover.

"Don't try to open it," she said to him. "It's locked." Isabel joined him and lighted the cover.

"You got the key?" he asked.

"Of course. How d'you think I got into the barracks in the first place?" She took out a key and unlocked the cover. "This cover is big, we'll have to use our backs to open it. Okay?"

"I'm strong enough," he said.

"Good... let's do it...!"

At the same time, they used their backs to make the cover move up, then aside. Then they used their hands to enlarge the opening. Isabel got out first, then Charlie.

They were now outside the barracks, in a dark alley. The sun had gone down. They could hear the noise from the crowd packed all around the base, but they were beyond or behind that too.

They closed the opening and Isabel locked the cover back, immediately after there was a loud noise, very close. A garbage bin, falling down. Then another. Then another.

Charlie and Isabel looked around, flabbergasted. All of a sudden they were surrounded. By four people, four young adults, all white. Three men, one woman.

"Hello Isabel…" one of the men said.

Isabel looked at the one who'd just spoken. And recognized him, with round eyes. "Ron!" she exclaimed, dumbfounded.

"I'm glad you didn't forget me," Ron said, grinning. "I've been after you for a pretty long time. But I'd never seen you handling a manhole cover and disappearing under the ground before. And you did it just today, close to that military base, with that kid in it, so we could guess that something was up."

"You know these people?" Charlie asked Isabel.

"Look at what you brought to us!" the woman said. "The teenage genius from nowhere!"

Isabel's reaction was immediate, at lightning speed she took out a small gun and put it to Ron's head. "Don't move!" she shrieked.

Ron and the others froze immediately.

"Don't you touch him! Back off!" Isabel's loud voice was heard by Laura, who was at the end of the alley, in some distance. She had seen Charlie and Isabel emerging from under the ground, as she expected them to do so. But she had stayed motionless at the sight of the others, not knowing what to do.

She started to move to them.

"Shit," Ron said, his grin wiped away. "I guess I forgot who I was dealing with."

"*Hey!*" Laura called from a distance, starting to run to them. They all turned their heads.

"Laura…" Isabel whispered. This was another appearance she hadn't expected any more than the others'. Neither had Charlie.

"No…" he whispered in his turn.

Ron took the opportunity; at lightning speed he took out another gun, and fired at Laura.

The bullet hit her at point blank, she was brutally thrown backwards and fell heavily on her back.

"*No!!*" Charlie yelled.

Immediately, before Isabel could react, Ron put his gun to her head. "Drop it," he said.

"How could you…?" Isabel couldn't believe he'd been able to shoot a total stranger. She didn't know him as well as she thought she did.

"Laura!" Charlie started to run to Laura.

"Stay here, you!" Ron roared to him.

One of the two other men ran after Charlie; Isabel saw him, she quickly moved her gun to him and fired. The man dropped, fatally hit in the back of the head. She immediately put the gun back on Ron. And Charlie kept running to Laura.

This was something totally unexpected by Ron as well. He didn't react.

"You *did* forget about me," she said to him, coldly.

Ron was so shocked that he needed a moment to say something else. "Tell the boy to come back here!" he finally said to the two others.

"Certainly not," Isabel retorted. "You think people are deaf? They heard the gunshots."

The two others didn't move, paralyzed with fear, certainly not wishing to get shot in their turn.

Charlie got to Laura. She was barely conscious. The bullet impact was bleeding a lot.

"Laura... you're okay?" Charlie asked, his voice shaking.

"You leave," Isabel said to Ron, "and you take the other two with you."

"Oliver, Sylvia, get the boy back," Ron said. "I'll watch her close."

"Laura..." Charlie said.

Laura recognized Charlie and smiled weakly, with relief and happiness. "I... I'll live," she said.

"Anyone that moves... gets it too!" Isabel screamed, frantically.

Ron made one step towards her. "*Go!!*" he ordered Oliver and Sylvia. "Don't you dare move a fuckin' muscle..." he said to Isabel, enraged, ready to shoot. But so was she.

Oliver and Sylvia moved to Charlie, watching Isabel over their shoulders.

Charlie was holding Laura's hand. "You'll be okay," he said to her. "You'll be all right."

"Charlie, take... take my phone..." she articulated.

Charlie looked around and saw the small mobile

phone on the ground, not far from her. He picked it up immediately.

His eyes came back to her right away, he could hear her saying: "Give it to her…" before she lost consciousness.

"Laura… Laura…?" Then he was grabbed from behind. "*No!! Laura…!*" he barked in despair.

He was taken to the other end of the alley as he kept yelling, so Oliver put his hand on his mouth to make him kind of silent.

"You'll pay for what you just did," Ron said to Isabel, calmly. "Let's go."

Isabel looked around and saw people watching the scene, on both sides of the alley. She immediately put her gun down and they went to a car parked nearby. There was somebody behind the wheel.

They all got in; as the car rolled away there were sounds of sirens approaching. Somebody outside the alley had called 911. The crowd was already pouring into the alley from both sides, but it was also staying carefully away from the two bodies.

VII

Charlie and Isabel were on the back seat of the car which was rolling normally. It was not being chased. It was a large car that could hold six people. Oliver and Sylvia were also on the back seat, on the left side, while Charlie and Isabel were on the right one. Ron was on the passenger's seat.

"Where's Ferris?" the driver asked.

"He's gone," Ron said. He was glaring at Isabel, as if he wanted to kill her with his own eyes.

"Gone where?"

"To heaven. She shot him."

"What?" The driver almost released the wheel.

"Didn't you hear?" Isabel said.

"D'you wanna see the murder weapon?" Ron asked him, then, without waiting for the response, he moved quickly and put his gun on Isabel's head. "Give me your gun," he said, coldly.

The driver was caught off guard by this, like the others, and he lurched. Fortunately, without losing control of the car.

"Hey, don't start this shit again!" Sylvia cried.

191

"Ron, put it down, man! That's enough!" Oliver said.

"Shut up!" Ron barked. To Isabel: "Give it to me. If you don't wanna die now. One way or the other, I'll get your gun."

Isabel didn't say anything, and she didn't move right away. She finally obeyed, but only after ten very long seconds.

"Could you put that away now? Please?" Sylvia said loudly.

Ron didn't put his gun down right away either. He kept it put right to Isabel's head. Isabel didn't move, neither did Charlie. Both were frozen. But Isabel didn't shut her eyes. The gun was so close to her face that she couldn't really see it. She was looking at Ron, straight in the face.

Ron finally put his weapon down, very reluctantly. And he showed Isabel's to the driver before getting rid of it through the window.

"She did him..." Ron said to the driver, snapping his fingers, "...just like that."

"So?" Isabel said, shrugging. "You should be happy for him."

"You better shut the fuck up," Ron said, furiously. "Don't say nothing more. You've done enough already."

"Don't curse in front of your Lord."

"Keep going this way, bitch."

"What are we gonna do about it?" the driver asked.

Ron looked at Charlie... and met a furious glare.

"Don't know," he said. He turned round to avoid the glare.

Charlie took the opportunity. He discreetly passed Laura's cell phone to Isabel, who took it.

*

The night had fallen.

The ambulance and police vehicles were at the scene. The ambulance was inside the alley, the police cars outside.

Laura was lying on a stretcher, itself lying on the ground. Her body was not covered. Some ambulance men were around her, working on straps.

Back in the alley, Stuart was struggling to get through the crowd, trying to figure out what was happening. He finally reached the edge and saw it. And could recognize Laura immediately, despite the workers around.

"Laura…" he whispered. He tried to have a better look, to make sure. "Laura!" he shrieked. He emerged from the crowd. "*Laura!*"

A policeman stopped him right away. "What the hell do you think you're doing?" he asked fiercely.

"I know this woman…"

"Laura Ingrams, yeah," the policeman confirmed, without being asked to. "You really know her?" he asked.

"How is she?"

"Who are you? Are you connected?"

"Er…"

"Are you her husband? Or brother?" This cop

apparently hadn't read the newspapers or watched television. Or he didn't care.

"No, but…"

"Then stay away. Please."

"Tell me how she is!"

"There's nothing to see and nothing to know," the cop said. "Now back off."

There was nothing more Stuart could say, so he backed off, very reluctantly. Then he turned his head and saw another stretcher lying on the ground. With another body on it, this one totally covered with a white sheet.

From this he understood that Laura was not dead.

He started through the crowd again, heading to his car that was parked nearby.

Soon Laura was taken into the ambulance, its back doors were closed and the vehicle left the alley and rolled away, blowing its siren, heading downtown.

*

Nobody was talking in the car. Charlie was looking down. Isabel was looking at him.

Ron turned to them. "Boy?" he said to Charlie, who showed absolutely no reaction. "Who was that woman?" Ron asked him.

"You'll find out on TV," Isabel answered for Charlie.

"We don't watch TV," Ron retorted.

"Oh yeah. I forgot."

"So?" Ron insisted.

Isabel stayed quiet. Charlie didn't answer either but he looked up at him.

"Who's this?" he asked Isabel.

"My ex-boyfriend," Isabel said.

"Really?" Charlie said, stunned. "Him?"

'Another trap,' he thought at once.

"We were pals, two years ago," she explained. "I was 15, he was 19. Back then I was still the typical stupid unconscious tart who gets involved with any boy she can find, without even trying to know the slightest thing about him. But I wasn't that stupid."

"You were," Ron said ironically.

"When I found out he was part of a cult group of loonies, I walked."

"Say that again if you can," Sylvia said to her.

"Say what?" Isabel said, turning to her.

"That loony stuff of yours, about us."

"Loony, loony, loony!"

Sylvia rushed at her but Oliver stopped her and controlled her. "I'll get you for that, you bitch!" Sylvia was shrieking. "You fuckin' killer!"

"Enough, you two!" Ron said severely.

"You should muzzle your whores," Isabel said to him.

"I will muzzle *you*. And tie you up. Nobody walks away from me."

"I already did," she said. "And I will again."

"What is that cult about?" Charlie asked.

Isabel turned to him. "You don't wanna know," she said.

"He will see," Ron said back immediately. He

195

turned to Charlie: "You might find it interesting. Who knows?"

"You guys leave him alone!" Isabel suddenly shouted.

"Hey, please… shut up."

"Stay away from him."

"Or what? What are you gonna do? What's gonna happen if I touch him? Judgement Day? End of the world? That's all I'm asking for."

"That's what I'm talking about."

"Take it easy," Charlie said. "He won't hurt me."

"He's not the group leader," Isabel specified.

"He's behaving like he was."

"He's the second. I mean I guess he still is."

The car entered another alley (a deserted one, in the dark) and stopped after some distance.

"All of you get out on the left side!" Ron said to everybody.

They all got out from the left side, the driver excepted, who stayed behind the wheel, since he was supposed to hide the car somewhere; as Isabel got out she activated something on Laura's cell phone, keeping it carefully hidden in her closed hand, without anybody seeing.

They entered an old building through a back door.

*

Laura had been admitted to the same hospital she had visited a couple of days before, after she found Charlie on the beach. She was alive and already having surgery.

Paul and Stuart were sitting in the waiting room, on the ground floor, a good distance away from each other. They were not talking, but they were sometimes having exchanged glances. They seemed to be wondering what to say, and when, and which one was supposed to talk first. The result was that they didn't say a single word.

The commander made an appearance. He was looking very dismayed. "Hello, Paul…" he said.

"Hey, little soldier," Paul said to him. He stood up and they shook hands. Stuart remained seated, like a total stranger.

"How is she?" the commander asked.

"She lost a lot of blood. But she's having an operation, so I guess she'll be all right."

"No more details?"

"Still waiting for that. They're working on her."

"All right," the commander nodded. "What about the boy?"

"You should know," Paul said, unhappily. "He was in your barracks. What happened?"

The commander had a seat. "I'd like to ask my daughter about that," he said. "I guess both of them have been abducted by the folks who shot your wife."

"You only guess? It's obvious. Don't you have any idea who they can be?"

"No. Except those guys she was with some time ago but I can't be sure."

"What guys?"

"She told me a little about one of them only, but I could guess it was bad." The commander had a sigh, then: "A cult, non-religious group."

"She was really part of such a group?"

"To be honest with you... I don't know," the commander said, shaking his head. Then he noticed Stuart, who was watching them. "Who's that?" he asked.

Paul sighed in his turn. "I'd like you to meet..."

He interrupted himself. Somebody else had just showed up. Detective Robredon. "Gentlemen, I have some news," he said.

Paul and the commander turned to him, ignoring Stuart again.

"That young boy who's been shot dead has just been identified," Robredon announced. "His name was Ferris Johnson, and he's in our file of missing persons."

Paul and the commander looked at each other. "He was missing?" the commander asked, dumbfounded. At that moment worrying about his daughter more than he wished to.

"Who shot him?" Paul asked.

"We don't know," Robredon answered, "but we have analyzed both bullets. They're different. Fired from two different firearms. The bullet that killed the young Johnson was from a 22 calibre pistol."

"My daughter's," the commander said immediately.

"Sorry?"

"She's been carrying a small gun on her since the

very moment she broke with her nutty ex," the commander explained.

"That doesn't mean anything," Paul argued.

"It means she didn't expect those guys to show up at that moment, and she used her gun to try to protect Charlie. And herself."

"That makes sense," Robredon said.

"What was Laura doing there?" Stuart asked from somewhere.

They turned to him.

"Mister Dano," Robredon said. "Hello."

The commander then understood who Stuart was, and he glanced at Paul.

"Laura was supposed to see Isabel taking Charlie away, with no problem," he said. "That was part of the plan."

"And it went wrong."

"Many crazy people are after Charlie now, so after what happened inside the barracks, maybe I could have seen things coming. Maybe I should have been there with them."

"Maybe you couldn't," Stuart said.

"I don't know."

"Any more news?" Paul asked Robredon.

"We have their car's plate number. That's all we have for the moment," Robredon said. "We're working on it."

*

A door opened. It was a small door that was almost reaching the ceiling. Ron entered, having to bend over a little since the ceiling was way too low. The following ones had to do that too, except Charlie and Isabel, who discovered some kind of a small, low-ceilinged hall leading to a room, through a door.

"It stinks in here," Charlie said.

Isabel guffawed a little, despite the situation.

"Move in, all of you," Ron said. "Oliver, watch those two."

They moved to the door and entered a huge, rectangular room, also low-ceilinged. The whole place was sort of a mezzanine. A closed mezzanine, a half-floor in the building.

The room was filled with what was called the Group. About forty people, more or less young adults, smoking or not, drinking or not, most of them sitting on chairs, couches, or armchairs. The whole room was barely lit, with candles and gas lamps. There were no windows. On the whole, the room was messy, but not really dirty.

And the place was definitely a secret one.

As they moved in, the others stared at them, at Charlie, who was discovering all of this with much amazement. Isabel looked at him, watching the expression on his face.

"Now what?" Charlie said, turning to her.

"I wouldn't be surprised if they ask you to sit on that big chair and play some divinity," she said, not trying to be funny.

"Keep your mouth shut, please," Ron said.

Isabel didn't keep her mouth shut. "From where I am, I'd say you've grown bigger," she said.

"Much bigger," he corrected.

"Not that much. In a couple of years you've only become a real group. Nothing more."

"Tell me about it," he said, grinning.

"So you guys moved away?" she asked.

"We have all moved in here today. For tonight. And tomorrow. Maybe more days, if the kid's prediction is a fake. This place's been familiar to us for some time now." Ron turned to somebody else. "Master," he said to him, respect-fully.

Somebody was coming to them. A small man, old, grey-haired, with dark, penetrating eyes, an aquiline nose and some other worrying things on his face. Somebody you clearly couldn't live in society with. You could tell from a first sight. He was wearing a long, grey dress, and no cross. He stared at Charlie, examining him from head to toe.

"Hello, young man," he said to him. "We won't shake hands, not now. Maybe later. In another life." He looked at Ron. "Did you search them before you let them in here?" he asked him.

"I didn't, master," Ron said, caught off guard. This was something he'd never done before.

"Who is she?" the Master said, frowning.

"It's Isabel," Ron said. "You saw her once, two years ago, when I brought her in the first place. I just ran into her again, tonight. She was with him."

"Oh yes. Of course. Well, search her."

"Sure."

"I don't want his hands on me," she said categorically. To the Group Master: "Please call somebody else."

201

The Master didn't say anything to this, just nodding to Ron. Who searched Isabel, and didn't find anything. He nodded to him.

"Please follow me to my private rooms," the Master said.

As they did, Charlie noticed a big table in the center of the room. It had been placed upside down, feet up, with a big candle on each foot. There was a big, empty armchair in the middle of the table.

The Group Master entered his 'private rooms', in fact a single office, windowless as well. Ron, Charlie and Isabel followed, and Oliver stayed outside. The Master had a seat behind his 'desk'. Then he stared at Charlie again, without saying anything. This lasted a whole long minute. And the more it lasted, the more Charlie felt uncomfortable with the stare. Isabel took his hand and held it tight.

"Who are you?" the Master asked suddenly.

Charlie jumped a little. The question had been brutal. "Why?" he asked.

"Just asking."

"I guess I'm Charlie Bradshaw."

"You guess. You're not sure."

Charlie just shrugged, saying nothing.

"Where are you from?" the Master asked.

"Don't know exactly. From Arkansas, I guess."

"All right," the Master said, sounding and behaving kind of normally. "I won't bother you with this any longer. If you forgot everything about yourself, if you're kind of amnesic, it's okay. The only thing is, you lost your memory when you're not suffering from it at all. And I'm saying that when I'm no doctor. Not any more, I mean."

"He used to be a doc," Isabel explained to Charlie. "Not very good."

"Nobody's talking to you," the Master said to her. "One more disrespectful word and you leave the room." He turned back to Charlie. "Whatever happened to you, big hit on your head, tornado, disease, etc., it doesn't matter since nobody can find out for sure."

"What do you think happened to me?" Charlie asked.

"Whatever I or anybody else can say about that, you'll never be convinced. Right? Only you can definitely tell about who you are." He remained silent for a short moment. "I still believe your memory has somehow been erased and replaced with something else. Some gift, allowing you to see things nobody can normally see."

"So?"

"I need to check it out, about that earthquake you saw happening."

"What are you talking about?"

"You know it will happen, right?" Charlie didn't answer. The Master took this as a yes. "You do know," he confirmed. "You're the only one to know for sure. We need to know too. I need to know too."

"You mean you need to see it happening. Or not."

"Okay, you can put it that way. Out there nobody really wants or needs to know. Except the fanatics. Who want you to carry their cross."

"If it does happen you'll die, and everyone here will be dead too," Charlie said.

"Don't tell me you care about us. You don't know anybody here. You just came in."

"I don't want people to die around me!" Charlie protested. "Who do you think I am? I don't reason like you do. You hate people and society that much?"

"This society doesn't care about you," the Master said serenely. "They don't care about what you said. We do."

Charlie realized only now that he was trying to 'turn' him. "So for you that's why I'm supposed to stay here with you and let myself be killed? Because you care?" Charlie said, almost scandalized. "I don't wanna die."

"Why not? You have nothing to live for."

"That's not a good enough reason for you to take me down with you."

"You have nothing to live for and this society won't give you anything but always more pressure and trouble to deal with, all by yourself. But you have something that is way beyond this society. I wanna use it at least once."

"So?" Charlie said again, pretending not to know anything. But what he heard was beyond what he was expecting.

"So we're gonna stay here and wait until tomorrow. If that earthquake really occurs and destroys the city, as you said it would, it will make you the ultimate prophet."

"I told you they were loonies," Isabel said to Charlie.

She immediately turned to leave the room, so she wouldn't have to face the Master's anger. But Charlie grabbed her arm and kept her behind him.

"That's total nonsense," he said. "Do you see yourself as a prophet?"

"I used to…" the Master answered, "until yesterday, until you showed up. Until what you said."

"How did you hear about what I said?"

"Ron told me. That's why I need to find out. And die with some good certitude."

"You're crazy," Charlie said with good certitude.

"Don't say that."

"Do you really expect the ultimate prophet or whatever you may call him, to die tomorrow, under what's left of a collapsed building?"

"Jesus Christ was a prophet as well. And see what happened to him."

This made Charlie jump again, higher. "Hey…" he could say in a gasp.

"I know you're not the Lord. That is total nonsense. Nonsense typical from this society, when it loses control, when it thinks it has found some Messiah to rule it the way it wants. You're not the Messiah, you're just a lost kid with a gift but who still needs explanations, when the other kids here don't need any. Not any more."

"I guess, because they took your food for free?"

"From tomorrow they may start to take your food."

Charlie looked at him, incredulous. This was almost funny. "From where?"

"Think better."

"I'm not interested," Charlie said. "Let me out."

"Come on. You know we can't."

"I may be lost but I'm not crazy. I'm not interested in dying, especially in here, when I'm still looking for the good answers about myself. There are people out there looking for me anyway. People who care about me."

"Possibly." The Master was still as serene as he was when the conversation started. He was sure of himself. He seemed to know definitely what he was doing. "Whoever they are they don't care enough to find you. Not here, not until what you have predicted."

"What's making you so sure?" Charlie asked.

"I don't need your gift for that."

That was it.

There had been no mention of Ferris not being there any more, and there wouldn't be; Charlie had replaced him, he'd even done much better than that – so to speak.

*

Laura had been operated under general anaesthetic, so she was still unconscious as she was now lying on a bed, in a classical room. She had a thick bandage around her naked chest. Paul, Stuart, the commander and Doctor Sanford were in the room, all around her.

"The operation was a success," the doctor started. "She was lucky, the bullet hit her just between her lung and shoulder. Her spine is safe too. We had to work a bit on her scapula though."

"And?" Paul said. He was seated by his wife, the others were standing.

The doctor smiled, then he shrugged. "She'll be all right. She should recover consciousness this very night."

"Good," Paul said. "I want her out of here, first time tomorrow."

"I beg your pardon?" That Paul Ingrams was something, Sanford was seeming to think. Always making big, totally unexpected decisions, just like that...

"You heard me," Paul confirmed. "Evacuated."

"Evacuated?" the doc said, amazed. "How?"

"Don't you know how?"

"We have a helicopter but..."

"But what?" Paul asked. "Can't you use it?"

"I guess we can."

"So what's the problem? Look, I'll talk to the people in charge here, okay? Is this enough to make it easier?" He stood up. "I'm going to the police," he said, on his way out. "Are you coming?" he asked the commander.

"You should stay here," the commander said. "I can handle the police."

"We'll do it better together," Paul said.

"Three is better than two," Stuart said, on his way out.

"You should stay here," Paul said, stopping him.

"What?" Stuart said, stunned.

Paul grinned. "Show me you really care about her and stay here," he said. "I can guess you've always wished to be close to her, with my benediction, this is a good opportunity."

"Hey, wait a min…"

Paul ignored him and turned to the doc. "You got my number. Let me know about anything that happens, okay?"

"No problem," Sanford said.

Paul nodded and he left the room with the commander.

Five minutes later they were at the police station. They walked through the main room, up to an office with 'DETECTIVE ROBREDON – SAN FRANCISCO POLICE DEPARTMENT' on the door. They pushed it and walked in.

There was somebody else with the detective in the room. A man, standing close to the wall.

"Hello, gentlemen," Robredon said, "I was expecting you to come. Have a seat, please."

They took seats in front of Robredon's desk. Robredon shook his head. "For the moment we have no lead about where Charlie and your daughter could be," he said.

"Her name's Isabel," the commander said.

"All right. Isabel. But we're still looking."

"What about that car?"

"The license plate has led us to an address that is correct…"

"Where is it?" Paul asked, interrupting.

"In Lafayette."

"Out of town…" Paul almost whispered.

"Way out of town. These kinds of groups, which include missing people among their members, are usually found in the suburbs around the biggest cities, or in the countryside. Almost always in remote areas. Don't worry, the roads are blocked now, they can't leave downtown."

"Unless they did it before the roads were blocked."

"I don't think so. We've called the police there, we've given them the address, and they've found the place empty. I mean, totally empty. Absolutely nothing in it. A big, old house. We think they have moved to another place where the kids are right now and we can't find it."

"And this place may be somewhere downtown?" the commander asked.

"Yes."

"So?" Paul said.

"We have to wait," Robredon said, with a slight shrug.

"Wait for what?"

"For something to happen. For your wife to wake up, for instance. She may know something we don't know."

"What about this man," Paul said, pointing to the standing one, "does he know something we don't know?"

"He's a seismologist," Robredon said. "And he believes the kid is full of shit. That there's nothing to worry about."

"He will believe something else tomorrow," the commander said.

"I don't think so," the seismologist said, "since nothing will happen. Since that kid emerged from his coma he has brought nothing but chaos anyway."

"Because it's all his fault now!" Paul exclaimed angrily.

"The boy is sort of a psychic," the commander said. "Not you."

"A precog, to be more specific," Paul added.

The seismologist leant toward them, not believing. "A… a precog?"

"Yes, exactly," Paul said. "He has a precognition ability. Do you know what precognition means?"

"Did he prove it to you?" the seismologist asked.

"I saw it happening," the commander answered. "He was about to be evacuated from my base and he told us the helicopter he was in wouldn't be starting."

"Really?" the seismologist said, and Paul looked at the commander with surprise. He didn't know anything about this. The commander hadn't mentioned it until now.

"Yes, really. He said that *before* it actually happened. He knew it. Afterwards we tried with some of the other choppers we have and the same thing happened. Every time. So whatever you can say, it's useless since you don't know anything, when we do."

"You can't prove to us that the boy is wrong anyway," Paul added. "Not now."

"I can't prove anything, of course," the seismologist argued. "But…"

"Look," Paul interrupted, "I don't wanna hear your scientific jargon. I know you're a professional and I'm sure that everything you have to say is very interesting, but it won't get us anywhere. Because you can't prove that the boy is wrong. Listening to you would be a waste of time. All I want is find the boy and my friend's daughter as quickly as possible, earthquake or not. And since I kind of believe what the boy said, also have them evacuated, my wife included. That's all I'm asking for."

The seismologist took all this not too badly. Probably because Paul didn't give him the time to feel useless. "If we follow your reasoning," he said, "the whole city needs to be evacuated…"

"Exactly," Paul said immediately. "But what a single kid said is not enough to try to convince anyone in charge and make that happen, right? It would be a waste of time too." To Robredon: "How far exactly is that place you told us about?" he asked.

"You don't wanna go there…?"

"Why not?"

"I just told you, there's absolutely nothing in there!" Robredon said. "The whole place's been whitewashed…"

"Whitewashed?" Paul exclaimed, surprised. "By who?"

"Not by us," Robredon answered. "There's no cellar and no attic in the house. And again, it's totally empty. They checked everything, the floors and walls included, and they didn't find anything, no prints, no objects, no hideout, nothing at all. If you go there you won't find anything more."

*

Later that evening, the Group Master could find himself sitting in his armchair, in the middle of the room, as a matter of fact in the center of the table. It was totally dark inside, except for the candles on the table feet and for one single lamp dangling above the big man. Ron was sitting on the table right beside him.

Somebody played music on a guitar, another one beat on some drum as the big man started speaking.

"My children. My sons and daughters. Listen to my prayer. It's a prayer for your glory. For the glory of everybody in this room. We've come a long way, and we've waited a long time for this kind of thing to happen. A prediction was given this very afternoon by a lost kid just like all of you. A kid, alone in a world he's a total stranger to. In a world that never gave you anything, and that has nothing to give him. And this kid is here tonight. Among us. Among you, my children. Is this the will of some

Providence? No. *We* made it happen. And we need nothing and nobody to make things happen."

There was some applause. They knew the Master was just starting so it lasted only two seconds.

"Now... nobody outside is taking this young boy's prediction seriously. They're all continuing on like nothing will happen. Because they don't want to hear the truth. Because they want to feel so safe and secure that they can't believe that something serious may hit them. Because that prediction doesn't fit their small wishes and desires. Well, it does fit our only wish and desire, doesn't it?"

There was some more applause of approval, more intense. And more music.

"Join me in prayer. Let's pray for this prediction, this prophecy, to come true so we prove the whole world..."

"...Prove what?"

It was Charlie's voice. The Master turned to him, dumbfounded. "How dare you interrupt...?" he said, outraged.

"You'll be too dead to prove anything to anybody!" Charlie said loudly, with much conviction.

"They will all know that the world is not some cocoon that's been built especially to keep them safe from the worst disasters."

"And you're ready to keep all these anonymous people in here for that?"

"They are not anonymous people, they are my children!" the Master recited.

"Are you kidding?" Charlie retorted. "They're

not your children, they're just brainwashed puppets who swallow your crap."

The Master couldn't believe his ears. He turned to Ron, who hadn't moved an inch. The Master had to push him aside and Ron woke up. "Ron, would you and your friends take him away and keep him silent, until this is finished? Please?" Ron stood up. "Thank you," the Master added.

"Don't..." A hand closed Charlie's mouth, Ron came to him and he was taken away to the hall.

The Master continued and finished his speech, almost like nothing had happened, like Charlie hadn't said anything. "Let's pray for this prediction, this prophecy to come true, so all these people who are so convinced that nothing bad will ever happen to them, that they are protected from anything dangerous, are proved that they are not under any protection, that they are not the kings of the universe, elected to rule it until the end of time. My children, my sons and daughters, join me in prayer! Join me in prayer, for a journey to a different world, a perfect world filled with real people who know the truth! A world with plenty of things to be given to everyone! Pray with me!"

There was an explosion of joy and the music suddenly reached a top level. But they still had to stay down, seated, crouching, kneeling or lying on the floor. The ceiling was too low to allow them to stand on their feet.

VIII

In her bedroom, Laura was still unconscious. The doctor had been too optimistic, she hadn't recovered consciousness during the night.

At a little before 7.30 am, she opened one eye.

She looked around, checking the place she was in, and saw nobody around. It was the first time she was in a hospital as a seriously treated patient. She'd never been pregnant and seriously ill or wounded in her life, even as an athlete. She made a move and winced with pain. But she kept moving and finally pushed a button on the wall.

There were two women behind the main desk, one of them heard the signal and quickly found out where it was coming from. "Gentlemen?" she called. "Hey, gentlemen?"

Paul and the commander were sitting on benches in a corridor, on the hospital's ground floor, not far from the main desk, more or less sleeping. Paul had spent several hours at his wife's bedside, before finally joining the commander on the ground floor.

They didn't move so she came to them and slightly shook Paul's shoulder. He opened an eye at her. "I've got a signal from your wife's bedroom," she said to him.

Paul stood up almost immediately. "Thank you," he said to her. Then he shook the commander, who woke up in his turn. "Emergency, man!"

They both ran to the elevators.

Soon they arrived in front of her door, and they saw Stuart sleeping on one of the benches in the corridor, outside the room. They didn't go to him, and entered the room, going straight to her. She was still awake. Paul took her hand. "Honey... how are you doing?" he asked her softly.

"I'll be all right..." she said weakly, then: "where's Charlie?"

"Nobody knows," Paul said, shaking his head.

"He has my cell phone," Laura said.

"Really?" Paul's eyes lit up.

"I gave it to him."

"All right," he said after a two-second silence. "Thank you. I'll do what's necessary about this. I'll have to get you evacuated, is that okay to you?"

"Sure... sure," she said, nodding and smiling. "Hello, commander," she said, turning to him.

"Hello, Laura," he said, coming closer. "How d'you feel?" he asked.

She only made a gesture as a response.

"Where's the doc?" Paul asked.

"I'm calling Robredon," the commander announced. He took out his cell phone. Paul kissed Laura's forehead and left the room. The commander followed him out as he was dialling Robredon's office number.

Once back in the corridor Paul ran straight to Stuart, who was still snoring, and started shaking him. "On your feet, bubblehead!" he said harshly. "She just woke up and you..." He interrupted himself, walking away, looking for somebody else, finally managing to stop a nurse. "Get the doc here," he said to her. "I want one of your patients evacuated. Now."

Robredon was still in his office, on the phone, writing something down on a piece of paper.

"Okay... got it," he said. "Come quickly. I'll be in the basement." He hung up and left his office.

As he was running through the detective room he called around: "Get the lieutenant, send him downstairs. Do it now!"

He left the room and ran downstairs to another room filled with hi-tech computers and screens set high up on walls.

He walked to somebody sitting in front of one of the keyboards. "Hey Kevin..." he said to the guy.

"Yeah?" Kevin said. He was busy.

"Sorry for disturbing you, but I need you to locate a cell phone on your map." Robredon gave him the piece of paper. "This is the number," he said. "It's an emergency."

"No problem." Kevin typed the phone number and clicked 'Enter'.

The computer started working and after a couple

of seconds… *zoomed in* on a building based downtown.

"It's in there," Kevin announced.

"Where exactly? Which floor?" Robredon asked quickly.

"Er… the computer can't tell," Kevin answered. "But it's in there."

"Try to find the exact spot!"

"It's impossible. I can only provide the street address." Kevin pointed at it on the screen. "Here it is."

"All right." Robredon wrote the address down on the same piece of paper and left the room. On his way upstairs, he crossed the lieutenant.

"Yes, Detective, are you looking for me?" the lieutenant asked.

"We found where they are," Robredon announced. "The two kids."

"Oh… okay, good. I'll send all units there immediately."

"Ingrams and the commander are on their way up here."

"Go to the place. I'll get them."

On their way to the station, Paul, Stuart and the commander crossed plenty of police cars hitting the road, going the reverse way. Four small police helicopters were going as well.

As soon as they entered the place, the lieutenant called to them. "Over here, gentlemen!"

They ran to him and, as the lieutenant was walk-

walking down the stairs, they followed him down to the basement.

They came to the same guy in front of his computer, Kevin. "According to the cell phone, they are in this building," he said. "I got pictures of it from the surveillance cameras around. Look."

They all looked up, at three screens showing the building from different angles. The building was made of stone; it was looking rather old and was surrounded by skyscrapers, all of them in better condition.

"I need to call my men," the commander said. He stepped away to make his call.

"How did you find out?" Stuart said, curious.

Kevin looked at him. "Don't you know about the SpyPhone system?" he said. "We can trace any cell phone registered, from its call number."

"Great. To hell with privacy," Stuart said ironically.

"Come on, that kind of system's been out there for a long time. Everybody knows about it. It doesn't keep people from getting always more cell phones. They need to be watched and noticed. Some of them *want* to be watched and noticed."

"All right, all right," Paul interrupted. "Which floor are they on?"

"I don't know. It's not possible to say for sure."

"It should be!" the lieutenant said, showing amazement. "Shouldn't it?"

"It should, yes," Kevin approved. "Any system has its limits, but this one should show us the exact place."

"Is it possible to check the phone's hard drive, from this computer, through this system?" Paul asked.

"Sorry?" Stuart said. His voice showed he was visibly uncomfortable with the idea.

"Yes," Kevin said, looking at Paul. "It's possible but…"

"Do it," Paul said. "We may find something."

"Hey, you can't do that…" Stuart protested.

"The phone is *my* wife's, not yours. You don't have one anyway." Paul turned to Kevin. "Go ahead. It's all right."

Kevin started by checking the photos saved inside the phone's hard drive. Some of them were showing Laura and Stuart together, at different locations. At this sight, Paul and Stuart looked at each other, Stuart showing real embarrassment. Paul shook his head and sighed as the photos kept going one after another, showing nothing useful.

"Faster, jump faster than that!" Paul said, annoyed.

Kevin kept going, until the photo list ran out. Nothing helpful.

"Check the videos," Paul said.

"All right." Kevin opened the videos section. "There's only one film saved," he said. He checked the recording date, without thinking. "Recorded… yesterday." Then he checked the time, thinking a little bit. "Last night!" he added.

"Last night?" Paul could only repeat.

Kevin opened the video file and… something came up. Something unusual.

A film starting with a pair of feet getting out of a car, and in the dark.

"Laura didn't film that. She's never filmed anything in her life!" Paul said, then he looked at Stuart. "Did you ever see her filming anything with her mobile?" Paul asked him.

"Never, not once," Stuart answered immediately, shaking his head.

The film continued, following from the point of view of the person who was holding the device. Soon it came to a door and showed people walking to it. From behind, so they couldn't see any of their faces.

"Somebody else shot this," Paul said.

"It's them," the lieutenant followed.

"Incredible," Stuart almost whispered.

"Larry, come here!" Paul exclaimed. He was talking to the commander who didn't hear it, still away, talking on the phone.

The screen brightened as a light turned on inside a building after the door was passed, and...

"That was Charlie," Paul almost shrieked, "I saw him!"

"The three of you, go back to the hospital," the lieutenant said. "I'll handle this from here."

"Can't you record that and come along?" Paul suggested.

"Just go. Please. We don't have time for anything. Even for this." The lieutenant took out a radio and, as Paul, Stuart and the commander were leaving: "Detective... somebody special will help you out there. Don't go in any place without him. Got it?"

*

Many cars arrived around the building, their sirens shrieking like crazy. Almost all their doors opened and plenty of men in uniforms got out. Among them was one putting a special red helmet on his head. And Robredon, holding a radio.

"Lieutenant?" Robredon said into his radio.

The lieutenant's voice came out of the device: "*Are you there?*"

"Yes."

"*There's an alley, in the back, do you see it?*"

"We're going." He went in, followed by a group of policemen in uniforms. Among them was the one with the special helmet, with a very small video camera inserted. He was in the middle of the group.

Soon the police choppers showed up above the building.

Everybody inside the building's half-floor could hear the noise.

"What's that?" the Master asked, still showing no anxiety.

That noise definitely did not sound like an earthquake. Nothing was shaking. Charlie didn't say anything. The others didn't say more. They just waited, for the noise to fade away. But the noise didn't fade away. They still could hear the sirens from the cars. But there was something more to it.

That something was coming from the almost silent police helicopters, which were now standing by in the air, around the building.

Charlie could guess what was going on but he stayed silent. He thought that he'd just spent his very first night since he emerged from the coma. That hadn't really been the kind of night he'd expected to spend. The day before he had experimented a comfortable bed in a house (and in a hospital, when he was still in his coma, as Laura told him), and that night he had ended up on the floor, in a low-ceilinged, windowless mezzanine inside an antique building, surrounded by cranks. Absolutely no connection with his last night before the tornado – that night he spent with Veronica, the daughter of another military base commander. A night he had no memory of.

But he had an unclear memory of one dream he had last night, with another young girl in it, a teen blonde; he could remember only a small part of what they were doing together but this didn't stop him from wondering if that girl was part of his lost past or if he only imagined her. Also, he wondered if it would be possible for him to somehow reconstruct his past from dreams or pieces of them, in the future, whatever that future would be…

Two men in white overalls emerged on the outside, in the hospital's main yard, pushing a rolling stretcher with Laura's uncovered body lying on it, straight towards a helicopter – a medevac helicopter, used as an ambulance – about to take off, with Paul, Stuart and the commander around. Laura was suffering a lot but she wasn't complaining. The bearers put the loaded stretcher into the copter, then the three men got inside, the doors got closed and the helicopter took off with no delay.

Robredon entered the alley and waited. "Who's the guy that is supposed to join me here?" he asked into his radio.

"He'll be wearing a red helmet. Wait for him."

"How long?" As soon as Robredon said that, the guy showed up. With his helmet on, ready to be used. "What's so special with the helmet?"

"Can't you see what's on it? Let him go first. Then you guys follow him."

The lieutenant put the radio down and picked up a microphone. "Keep walking," he said to the helmet cameraman. "The door is grey."

Above him, among the screens, there were two of them, placed side by side, the one showing the film from Laura's cell phone, the other taking the helmet cam's point of view.

The helmet cameraman kept walking along the alley, the other guys behind him. Passing in front of doors from a distance. Then:

"This one! Try this one."

On the screen, Kevin and the lieutenant could see the helmet cameraman pointing a finger at the door.

"*That one?*" the helmet cameraman asked.

"Yes. I guess that's the one."

The man reached the door and… opened it.

It was dark.

"*Okay, let the police guys find the switch.*"

The others went inside behind the helmet cameraman, found the switch and turned the light on.

"Now you have to walk to the left," the lieutenant said. He had to watch both films at the same time, the one on the left screen which was already recorded and saved, the other one being broadcast live.

But Kevin was working too, providing good assistance.

The helmet cameraman walked along.

"Who's telling you where to go?" Robredon asked. He didn't know about the film from Laura's phone.

The helmet cameraman didn't respond. Maybe because he was too busy to be able to hear the question.

"Yeah, keep going…" the lieutenant was saying into the microphone.

He saw, on both screens, the guys reaching the main hall, then, on the left screen, another door being opened.

"That door. Go open it. There's a flight of stairs behind it."

The helmet cameraman opened the door and walked in.

"*Wait. Right here. On your left.*"

The stairs didn't start immediately after the door was opened. There was about a yard and a half between.

The helmet cameraman looked left and saw nothing right away. "What?" he asked.

"*Something here. Like another door.*"

"I don't see anything."

"Who are you talking to?" Robredon asked.

"*Tell the detective to keep his mouth shut.*"

"The lieutenant's telling you to keep your mouth shut," the helmet cameraman told Robredon, without smiling.

"The lieutenant..." Robredon said, nodding. "Nothing wrong with asking."

"He's also saying there's a door here. Check it out."

This made Robredon react. "A door?" he asked.

"Yes," the helmet cameraman confirmed.

There was an indentation in the wall, from the floor to the ceiling, but nothing allowing to spot a door. No handle, no lock, nothing. The wall was clear.

"Do you have a clue?" the helmet cameraman asked.

"I can't tell, the other video doesn't show anything," the lieutenant said.

He saw Robredon getting closer to the wall. And touching it with his fingers.

"There's something all right," he heard Robredon saying. *"I can feel an air current."*

"Blow up the door," the lieutenant said.

"He's suggesting we blow up the door," the helmet cameraman said to Robredon.

"Wait…" Robredon started pushing on the wall, on its both sides, with his both hands. Nothing moved. "It needs to be pulled," he finally announced. "And we can't do that."

"You guys just blow it up!"

"Same suggestion," the helmet cameraman said.

"He doesn't want them to hear us," Robredon argued.

"I think they heard us already."

"Look, the elevator system is right behind that door… he doesn't want it wasted either."

Since last night's collective prayer the Group members weren't able to do anything else but eat, sleep and wait. And pray more, for most of them. Charlie was waiting as well. He remembered what he said to Laura about his prediction, as he was emerging from his coma, and how vague he'd been. But now he was sure. And of course he knew what was going to happen in this place. The info was clear; it was even better than the one that came through his mind once he'd got inside that army base.

Charlie and the Master hadn't talked once since the speech. They didn't have to; the Master was trusting Charlie enough about his prediction (only that), and he was over trusting himself about the rest.

The sirens were still sounding from the outside. Along with that weird little noise, like from a low vacuum cleaner. Ron walked to the wall, the one leading to the outside. "They're still out there," he said after a short moment. He got frustrated enough to add, upset: "And we can't see anything!"

"You could blow up the wall," Charlie suggested.

Ron turned to him. "That's a good idea, but we don't accept weapons of any kind. Explosives included."

"You used a gun last night," Charlie retorted.

"Outside, of course. And I had to. The little witch had her gun on me."

"You shot somebody else."

"No weapon use allowed within the Group, young man," the Master recited.

"But Isabel didn't know it," Ron added, "I guess that's the reason she got the gun after she walked away from me. To protect herself from us, when we don't use anything harmful."

"No shit," Charlie said. To the Master: "What if somebody comes in here?" he asked him.

"That's not gonna happen," the Master said, full of self-confidence.

Right at this moment there was the sound of an explosion. It was strong enough to make them all get down on the floor.

Robredon, the helmet cameraman and the others all had had to get away from the door before it exploded.

Then they all went back inside. There was smoke all around so they could hardly see the dark emptiness beyond the door.

"Be careful," the lieutenant said, "watch your steps after the door, I think there's nothing to walk on!"

He could clearly see that dark emptiness on the left screen.

"Roger that!" the helmet cameraman said. To Robredon: "Nothing to step on beyond the door!"

"Take your right, on the wall there's sort of a ladder going up and down."

"Which way do we have to go?" the helmet cameraman asked.

"Up. Hurry, they've definitely heard that."

"What the hell was that?" Ron asked, not understanding.

The explosion sound was still echoing all across the place, shaking it hard.

"This is from inside the building!" The Master's

certitudes started to falter. He looked at Charlie, who still wasn't saying anything. So he stood up and walked to him. "You tell me what's happening," he said to him.

"You said you didn't need me for that!" Charlie retorted.

"Ron, search him."

As Ron moved to Charlie, a very small door opened outside the place, in the corridor. The helmet cameraman appeared and started moving inside, followed by Robredon.

"Okay, keep going…"

Behind Robredon the first police officers appeared in their turn, knocking their heads on the low ceiling as they stood up.

"It's a half-floor, not registered," Kevin said to the lieutenant. "That's the reason I couldn't get the exact spot right away."

The lieutenant nodded. He also quickly estimated, from the left screen, that that half-floor was between the ground and first floors of the building, and he shuddered. An earthquake would probably blast the bottom floors, before all the ones above collapsed upon them. Nobody on the bottom floors would stand a chance.

Then he remembered what Robredon had reported to him about the probable kidnappers. A non-religious cult group. Which might have taken the boy's prediction as seriously as possible.

Potential candidates for a mass suicide.

He shuddered again.

"Check the girl again," the Master ordered Ron.

Ron walked away from Charlie towards a corner of the room and got to Isabel, who was 'sitting' there on the floor, gagged, her hands tied behind her back, her feet tied as well. Since the night before Charlie never could spot her in the dark, and he never could get to her since the gas lamps had been turned back on. Ron forced her back on her feet, put her against the wall, then he untied her feet so she could stay balanced and searched her. Like before he didn't find anything... then he saw her thick hair and checked it...

...and found Laura's micro mobile phone.

The helmet cameraman was walking along the corridor, passing more and more small, closed doors, until:

"Got it. That's the one."

The helmet cameraman signaled Robredon, showing him the door. Robredon did the same to the first policemen behind him.

"You've led them to us!" Ron said to her, angrily.

Isabel was still gagged, her hands were still tied behind her back when he punched her hard in the face.

"Hey! You bastard, don't you..." Charlie said, furious, but he couldn't go any further – as she collapsed, the police broke into the place. They quickly passed the empty hall and reached the main room, their guns pointed at the Group.

"Nobody move!" a policeman screamed.

"Everybody freeze! Everybody!" another one yelled.

They all did, except the Master who quickly pulled out a gun and put it on Charlie's head. It was the same gun Ron used to shoot Laura.

"*You* freeze!" he barked.

In the end nobody could freeze. Because everything started quaking. Hard.

*

Among the helicopters standing by in the air around the building was a big, white one with a red cross on it. It was the flying ambulance. Paul, Stuart and the commander were inside – so was Laura, lying half unconscious on the floor.

They all could see, feel and hear the earth shaking – except Laura who couldn't see.

"Oh, my…!" Paul exclaimed, highly shocked. He looked around and saw the whole city 'vibrating'. Laura could barely react.

"…my God! Isabel!" the commander screeched, starting to panic.

All those who were standing lost their balances. Charlie went down to the floor – so did Ron – as the Master involuntarily fired his gun. The recoil, added to the quake, made him drop the weapon.

The bullet hit the ceiling, close to the policemen who fired in the empty – they were unbalanced, too. The shooting forced everybody sitting on the floor to lie down.

Still, more policemen came in but they were immediately cast across the place. Nobody had control.

"Everybody out!" the lieutenant shrieked.

He and Kevin rushed out.

It was still shaking all over, in spite of that, Charlie managed to half stand, making his way to the police, but the Master saw him. He started looking around for his gun. He spotted it and closed his hand around it, but as he was about to use it, someone grabbed his arm. It was one of his own 'children', a young man, around 25.

"No! I can't let you do that!" the 'son' said.

The Master got rid of the guy, then he managed to put the gun to Charlie's back and pulled the trigger. *Click!*

"Shit…!" he cursed. He pulled the trigger again, once, twice more. With the same clicking result.

As Charlie joined the police, the Master checked the gun; he'd forgotten to cock it. He did it and aimed again but… one of the cops shot him first, just before he could fire. He was cast backwards, the gun released from his hand again.

"Everybody out!" Charlie yelled.

Among the Master's children, everybody was

shaking but nobody was really moving. Ron excepted. He 'ran' to the police and the exit.

The quake stopped.

Charlie went to Isabel, who was lying unconscious on the floor, gagged, her hands tied behind her back. He seized her. "Help me…" he said.

Another cop grabbed Isabel's body and they went to the exit. But Robredon stood there, looking at all the people lying on the floor, not moving. Sprawled zombies. "Come on, you must get outta here!" he exclaimed. "All of you!"

None of them showed any reaction. Nobody came to him. Almost nobody even looked at him.

Then Robredon looked up, at the low ceiling. Damaged enough to collapse at any time.

He left.

They reached the door, then the ladder, going the reverse way down. There they had a bad surprise: because of the earthquake, the elevator had twisted, and was partly blocking the way to the door on the ground floor. It was impossible to reach the exit.

"Shit, it's blocked!" said the policeman leading the way.

"Get inside the elevator!" Robredon said to him.

The policeman got it, he stepped on the elevator and opened the top. Then he jumped inside. "It's still working!" he announced loudly, after a short moment. "Get in, now!"

They all did; they had to do it quickly, before the

elevator got called. Which was exactly the thing that happened. The elevator started to move up.

The policeman pushed the alarm button and the elevator stopped as the alarm started to ring. "Come on!"

One after another, they got in, jumping on the top of the elevator, then jumping into it. There were eleven of them: Charlie, Robredon, Isabel, Ron, the helmet cameraman and six police officers.

The first policeman pushed the alarm button again, the sound stopped. Then he pushed the number 1 button. As the elevator moved to the first floor… there was an aftershock. Everybody got caught off guard.

The door still opened on the first floor. They all managed to get out of the terribly unstable elevator.

"We need to find the stairs!" Charlie said through the noise.

"No!" Robredon screamed. "Let's get to the windows!" He opened a door, then he ran across an empty room to one of the windows, and saw some helicopters in the air, standing by, as expected. He opened the window and waved to them, shrieking: "Hey! HEEEEEEY! Over here!"

One of the co-pilots saw him and Charlie, who had joined Robredon at the window. "We've got two people waving to us from the first floor," the co-pilot said in his micro. "We're going."

A voice uselessly said back: "It's them! Go!"

One helicopter, a police one, moved to Charlie, Robredon and the others, its top rotor blades being retracted so they couldn't hit the building – an important detail that Robredon knew about; soon it was close enough for them to get inside. Isabel, still unconscious, was taken inside first, then Charlie, Robredon, the helmet cameraman and the cop who had carried Isabel on his shoulder, followed. Until the helicopter was too full to take more.

"Let's move!" Robredon ordered the pilot.

The copter flew away, quickly replaced with another one, and the pilot had his top rotor blades redeployed as soon as he was a safe enough distance away from the building. But in the meantime Charlie turned around and looked at the shaking building. He saw only police officers in uniforms inside. "Where's Ron?" he said to himself.

"Tell everybody the two kids are safe," Robredon added, this time to the co-pilot.

The co-pilot did.

Charlie touched Robredon's shoulder. "Where's Ron?" Charlie asked him.

"Who?"

"The boy who was with us, in the elevator. He's the one who shot Laura."

The earthquake was still raging as Ron emerged from the building, through the front door. Alone. He had turned away from the group after the elevator reached the first floor and had made his way down, through the stairs.

He looked around him. And saw quaking chaos.

The police cars were all gone, but there were still some helicopters standing by in the air.

"Fuck me..." he whispered. He started to walk, trying to make his way through multiple things going down around him, trying not to get crushed.

Behind him, two of the other cops who were about to get inside the second helicopter, and who were ordered to go back for Ron, emerged out of the building the same way and 'ran' after him.

The Group Master was crawling his way through the low-ceilinged corridor to the exit, his teeth clenched. Crawling like a slug as he was leaving a thick trail of blood behind him, on the floor, from his bullet wound. He reached the way out, only to find it blocked by the shaking elevator.

He was trapped.

Ron was so busy trying to keep his balance while walking that he didn't notice the cops. Until he was grabbed from behind and forced down to the shaking ground.

"Now easy boy..." the first one said.

"Wh..." Ron sounded, flabbergasted.

"You're under arrest..." the second cop said to him. They were acting like nothing was happening around them. Like professionals.

"You're crazy! Let's get outta here!"

"You have the right to remain silent..." the first one recited.

"Everything you say can and will be used against you," the other one followed.

"I have only one thing to say now, get me back on my feet!" Ron cried.

"Shut up! Don't tell us how to do our job –"

As they cuffed Ron's hands behind his back, a helicopter got to them, not touching the quaking earth, they all boarded it and flew away.

*

The streets of San Francisco were cracking all across the city. As well as the high buildings downtown were cracking and breaking. The streets were swarming with people, all over the city, unable to do anything but yell and protect their heads with their hands and watch their steps to stay away from the cracks – and if possible, dodge things going down all around them, until the quake was over. So were of course most of the buildings and houses, with people being at home, or inside offices, hospitals, museums, etc., unable to move, unable to do anything but scream and pray for the places not to fall apart and bury them.

The US Air Force base was the only public place in town that had been totally evacuated. The evacuation order had been given by the commander from the surveillance room, at the police station. None of the sabotaged choppers had been fixed so they were still there like green, useless cockroaches. All the vehicles were gone. The buildings got progresssively destroyed, with nobody inside and outside. But they didn't collapse completely.

Some of the buildings downtown, especially the oldest and most fragile ones, as well as the smallest ones, collapsed like sand castles, including… the one where Charlie and Isabel had been held.

The Master was still trying to pass the elevator's bottom side… impossible. It was more and more unstable, shaking all around. And his bad condition – he was suffering and bleeding more and more – wasn't allowing him to move properly.

Inside the room his children were sitting on the ground, waiting for what they believed was their 'destiny'.

There was a sudden big crack and everything on the half floor exploded in a deafening noise.

The building's very bottom had just blown up and the whole building went down with it.

Part

THREE

From where he was, Charlie could see what he already saw in his vision, as he was emerging from his coma in the Ingrams' rented house: San Francisco, as a field of burning and smoking ruins. The dusty clouds were thick enough to cover the sun and block its beams, like a normal cloud would. Even if most of the buildings had resisted and didn't fall, they were all wrecked. That was what the people could more or less notice after the quake ended; among them, a delivery boy who was still holding a pack of newspapers, one of the last ones still being printed. His clothes and shocked face were covered with white and grey dust.

After a while Charlie looked away toward Isabel, who still hadn't regained consciousness.

"It's better for her," Robredon said. "It's better for her not to see this."

Robredon looked at the other choppers flying around and his eyes met the San Francisco Bay Bridge that was still shaking, even though the quake had ended. The traffic was now stopped due to the too many collisions. The Golden Gate Bridge was on the other side.

"What about Laura?" Charlie asked.

"Don't worry about her, she's safe."

"You mean she's alive?" Charlie asked, his heart beating faster.

"Yes. She's okay. She's in the medevac."

"Medevac?"

"A flying ambulance. That helicopter." He showed it to Charlie, pointing a finger. "We're heading to another hospital. In Sacramento."

"No layover?"

There was a pause as Robredon was coming to an answer. "It can be negotiated," he finally said.

The co-pilot was handling a newspaper, the same one the delivery boy was dealing with on the ground. It was a morning issue, which came out just before the earthquake started. The co-pilot had been able to snatch it from a tied pack before he entered the chopper.

"Detective," he said, and he handed Robredon the paper. Robredon took it.

The headlines were 'JESUS TAKEN'.

He didn't read the article and didn't show the paper to Charlie.

*

In the next ten minutes, the helicopters had passed Oakland and were flying over the portion of desert that separated Oakland and Berkeley from Sacramento.

After some time, two of them suddenly went down and landed in the desert – the one from the hospital and the police one with Charlie and Isabel inside. They did it close to each other, while the other helicopters kept flying away.

Charlie got off the police one, the commander off the other chopper. They ran to each other in the wind of dust pulled up by the choppers landing. There was almost no noise. They came towards each other and shook hands.

"She's okay," Charlie said to him, without having to cry it out. "She's been punched in the face, by her ex-boyfriend, but she's okay."

"I'll kill him before they lock him up," the commander said. "Thanks for taking care of her."

"It was reciprocal. She took care of me."

"Laura is recovering more quickly than we thought. She's been yelling for you."

Charlie nodded. "I'm on my way. Thank you, commander…"

"See you, young man."

They shook hands again then went their separate ways, trading helicopters.

*

Laura was clearly awake. Her right arm was in a sling. As she saw Charlie coming in, she almost half stood up.

"Good morning, Charlie," Paul said to him, smiling.

"Mister Ingrams…"

It was the first time Paul and Charlie were talking to each other.

"I'm very happy to meet you and speak with you at last, boy," Paul said, smiling.

"My pleasure," Charlie said, shaking hands with him, smiling back. "I don't know how to thank you for your protection."

"We'll talk this over later, okay?"

"No problem."

Then Charlie shook hands with Stuart.

"Hello, young man…" Stuart said.

"How d'you do?" Charlie had never seen that guy before and didn't ask who he was. He would know in time.

He went to Laura.

"Charlie…" she said, holding out her left arm to him, and they hugged each other warmly. She started sobbing.

"You're all right?" he asked her.

"I'm feeling much better now." She was looking so happy to see him safe and sound. Enough to forget about her own clinical condition.

"I thought they'd killed you," Charlie said.

"So did I. But I don't get wasted that easily."

"I can see that."

"Maybe getting shot was my punishment for leaving you behind," she said. "I'm so sorry, Charlie."

"Please don't be," Charlie said. "You were absolutely right."

"I was?"

"Yes."

"You know what?" she said. "I'm happy it didn't work out." They laughed and hugged each other again.

Then they felt more than they heard (from the wind and dust rushing inside) the other helicopter almost silently taking off when theirs was staying down on the ground. Almost immediately there was no more noise.

Charlie looked over his shoulder, at the outside. "What's going on?" he asked.

"We're not going anywhere," Paul announced. "Not for the moment."

"Couldn't you predict this?" Stuart said.

"I did," Charlie said. "But I didn't expect the other chopper to leave without us."

"We'll wait," Laura said.

"What do you mean?" Charlie asked them. "Wait for what?"

"This is something the army didn't tell about, but after what happened to you in the barracks here, they brought your parents to Sacramento last night, for no charge," Paul explained. "And your parents just heard about the earthquake of course. They said they could feel it. They're worrying about you now. I mean worrying like crazies. They want to see you as soon as possible, in order to make sure about you and to know you're all right."

"My parents...?" Charlie said, dumbfounded.

"Yes. Your real parents, Charlie. From Arkansas. The Bradshaws. I could talk to them on the radio, on this very chopper. They're on their way."

"And we wanna meet them," Laura said. "Your real family."

"That means your parents, but not only them," Paul specified.

"You mean…" Charlie said.

"You'll see. They also told about a few guests."

Charlie stayed there, speechless. But not motionless. He got off the chopper again.

There was nothing and nobody around but silence. Even the air ambulance was mute.

Soon there was one single sound, coming from a distance, and Charlie got back into the helicopter. And went straight to Laura. "I'll help you out," he said to her. "Do you mind?"

"I don't," Laura said immediately.

"Hey, you do!" Paul protested.

Laura shook her head and she let Charlie help her out of the helicopter, from her left side. She could walk. Soon Charlie was joined by Paul and Stuart. The four of them got together off the copter, and stepped into the desert.

Another helicopter, with the US Army logo on it, was flying straight to them. Its doors were closed. It arrived close enough to them and stopped moving, and as it was slowly landing its doors opened, on both sides.

The first person to come off the helicopter was a pretty brown-haired lady. She was almost as old as Laura.

It was Charlie's little sister.